NEO

WERE ZOO BOOK TEN

R. E. BUTLER

Neo

Were Zoo Book Ten

By R. E. Butler

Cover by CT Cover Creations

Edited by Sarah Dawn Johnson

Thanks to Joyce, Shelley, and Ann for beta reading.

NEO (WERE ZOO BOOK TEN)
BY R. E. BUTLER

Gorilla shifter Neo feels like he's been waiting for his soul-mate forever, even though he's only twenty-six. He keeps himself busy during the day as a mechanic at Amazing Adventures Safari Park, where he and his fellow shifters live in secrecy from humans. But the lonely nights are getting to him, and he wonders when he'll meet the other half of his heart.

Danielle Fitzgerald knows her stepfather, Dexter, and his son, Khyle, are keeping something from her and her mother, but she can't figure out what it is. There's something off about both of them–and the group of men that work for their construction company. Against her dad's wishes, she takes a VIP ticket for the safari tour and finds herself entranced with one of the gorillas.

Neo knows the moment the vehicle with his soulmate stops in front of the gorilla paddock, and his beast can't wait to meet her. He knows it will take a while before he can share the truth of his shift with her, but what he doesn't count on is her stepfamily's secret. When the truth comes out, will Dani be able to stay with Neo at the park, or will her family steal her away before he can stop them?

CHAPTER ONE

Neo Wright sat behind the wheel of the blue camo-colored Jeep in the maintenance shed and turned the key. The electric engine started smoothly. "Damn, that's nice," he said.

"Isn't it?" Atticus said. He was Neo's alpha and the head of maintenance at the Amazing Adventures Safari Park where they both lived and worked.

"Lemme ask you something," Neo said.

"Sure."

"When you were first learning about maintenance, did you ever think there would be electric engines?" Neo had only been fixing vehicles since he was eighteen. He'd come to the park from Ohio where his mother's band of gorilla shifters lived in a small farming town. He'd never twisted a wrench in his life, but Atticus had taught him everything he knew about maintenance, and Neo had taken some classes at the local community college as well.

"Not in a million years," Atticus said with a smile. "I thought we'd have flying cars at some point, but the idea of an all-electric vehicle never crossed my mind."

"Well, if it had we'd be billionaires," Neo said.

"Indeed."

Neo turned off the engine and climbed out. The park used the Jeeps for the safari tours, which took patrons on a trail to see the animals that called the park home. Among the normal animals–giraffes, a cranky moose, deer, and antelope–were other shifter groups. There were seven gorillas who lived in a private area underneath the park, hidden from humans who didn't know shifters existed. Along with their group, there were other shifter groups who lived underground in separate private areas as well–wolves, elephants, bears, and lions.

Zane, Atticus's son, walked into the maintenance shed. "You're coming to the party, right?"

"We wouldn't miss it," Neo said.

"How you doing, Papa?" Atticus asked as he clapped him on the shoulder.

"Nervous as hell." Zane smiled broadly.

Zane was one of the first males in the zoo to find his soulmate in a human female–Adriana. She was five months' pregnant and they were having a party to reveal the gender of the baby. The whole band was going to be there, as well as Adriana's best friend, a human female named Celeste who was mated to a lion shifter named Jupiter.

"I gotta go, but don't be late." Zane disappeared, and Neo shook his head at his friend.

"He's so damn lucky," Neo said.

"Yeah. Him and Win," Atticus said. Zane and Win were the only two gorillas who'd found their soulmates in human females.

"Do you think you'll find your soulmate?" Neo asked as he hung the keys to the Jeep on a hook on the wall. He picked up the tablet to finish the report detailing the inspection he'd just done.

"I hope so. I don't regret having Zane with his mother. I wish she'd been my soulmate. We got along really well." Atticus joined him at the long counter and looked over the jobs that needed to be completed.

"You could've mated her, even if you weren't soulmates," Neo said.

Atticus shrugged. "We talked about it. It took her three months to get pregnant, but it wasn't like we dated during that time. She called me when she was ovulating so we could have sex. I liked her, but it was damn clinical. Not even a little bit romantic."

"She didn't want to raise Zane with you?"

"No. She was originally from Europe and had come to the States to visit family but had no intention of staying permanently. I didn't want to leave the States. When we agreed to have a child together to continue our species, we decided if we had a girl that she would raise her, and I'd raise a boy. After Zane was born, she moved back to Europe. We stayed in touch for a while, but eventually she found another male to mate, and we lost touch. Zane stays in touch with her, though."

Neo ran a hand through his hair. "I don't want that. My mom was telling me the other day about a female in her band who's looking to have a child. I don't want to have a baby with someone I don't love. Or not see my own kid."

"I believe when you make the decision to choose to wait for your soulmate, that you'll find her eventually. Going the route I did isn't for everyone, and it has its downside. I think you'll find her when the time is right."

"Soon would be good," Neo said.

"If only it were that simple," Atticus said. He glanced at his phone. "Why don't we call it a day and head to the party? I'm sure Zane could use some help setting up."

"Sounds good," Neo said.

He closed out the report and made a mental note for what he needed to complete the next day. Atticus closed and secured the main door of the maintenance shed and then lifted the hidden door in the floor. A staircase led to a locked door, which opened into the gorillas' private area. They could also access their area through a shed within their paddock on the safari tour, and through the employee cafeteria which was topside in the park.

Their private area was decorated to mimic the jungle. Their homes were built on fake trees made of concrete and steel, covered with a bark-like material that felt real, with branches covered in silk leaves. Each gorilla had his own house. Neo's had two bedrooms and two bathrooms, with a small kitchen and a family room with an electric fireplace. Today, the private area was set up with several round tables surrounded by chairs, and two tables for food.

"Hey, can you help bring the food from the market?" Zane said as he carried a table and set it behind a chair.

"I guess we're right on time to give you a hand," Atticus said.

"It would help me a lot," Zane said. He put the table down and opened the legs. "Adriana keeps trying to carry stuff, but she can't see her feet, and I'm worried she'll trip and hurt herself."

"We've got it, no worries," Neo said.

He and Atticus walked to the market, a central gathering place underground. The bears handled the food for the entire park–from the stands that sold food to park visitors to stocking the employee cafeteria with grab-and-go meals. Most of the park's residents ate meals in the market or had them delivered to their homes.

"Hi guys, what can I get you?" Jeanie, human mate of the alpha wolf Joss, asked as she finished boxing up a sandwich and sweet potato fries.

"We're here to pick up the food for Adriana and Zane's party," Neo said.

"Great, I'll grab it." She placed the cardboard container on the counter and said, "Cael?"

The elephant shifter strode up to the counter. "Thanks, Jeanie." He took the container and greeted Neo and Atticus.

"How's things?" Neo asked. Cael was the park's veterinarian and handled the normal, non-shifter animals.

"Pretty good. You guys?"

"Same old, same old," Neo said.

"I hear you. Maybe the VIP tours this weekend will bring in some soulmates."

"Maybe," Neo said.

Cael took his meal and said goodbye. Neo stared after him for a moment and then turned around. "Everyone's always so hopeful about the tours."

"It doesn't do anyone any good to give up."

"I know. I just wish we had more to show for it after running the tours for such a long time."

The alphas of each shifter group had gotten together over a year ago and decided to send out tickets to eligible males and females in the tri-state area. Each human got free entry and parking at the park as well as a private safari tour. All the shifters took turns being in their shifts during the tours which happened on Fridays, Saturdays, and Sundays year-round. Despite the many long hours he'd spent in his shift in the gorillas' paddock during the tours, and the many hundreds of unmated human females who'd gone by, he'd not found his soulmate among them.

So few soulmates had been found through the tours that many were giving up hope in them. And maybe Neo was among them. He wasn't sure if he was ready to call it a day with the tours or not. Because what if he decided it wasn't worth the trouble and he missed his soulmate?

Shaking his head to clear his thoughts, he accepted the large box that Jeanie brought to the counter.

"You okay?" Atticus asked.

"Just thinking."

"About your soulmate?"

Jeanie came back with another box. "Here you go, guys. Have fun at the party."

"Will do, thanks," Atticus said.

They turned away with their boxes, and Neo said, "Yeah, I'm tired of waiting for her, though."

"I wish I could see into the future and tell you how long you have to wait until you find your soulmate."

"That would be damn handy."

"You're not giving up, right?"

"No." Neo entered the code to unlock the door to their area and shouldered it open, holding it for Atticus. "It's hard not to want what Zane and Win have."

"Of course. You'll find her, I'm sure of it."

Neo nodded but didn't say what he was really thinking. That he wished he could just walk into the park and find her. Not someday. Today.

It wasn't in his control, though. No matter how much he wished he could meet her soon, he'd meet her when the time was right. He wasn't going to enter into a mating with a female who wasn't his soulmate, or contract with one to have a child. So if he had to wait, then he would. And he'd be the best damn mate in the universe to her.

If she'd just show up.

CHAPTER TWO

Danielle smoothed her black half-apron and checked that she had pens and business cards in one of the pockets. She looked at the station where someone would sit, where she'd help them find the perfect shade of lipstick or quad of eye shadow or recommend makeup brushes or moisturizer. She loved her job at Beauty, which she'd taken after she'd gone to cosmetology school for makeup.

When Dani was a teenager, she'd thought it would be fun to do makeup for television or movies, but then she'd done makeup for a wedding party when she was a senior in high school, and she'd been hooked. She didn't want a glamorous job like being a famous makeup artist in Hollywood, she just wanted to do special occasion makeup.

If only she could get a few more clients and grow her home business. Then she wouldn't have to stand on her feet in Beauty five days a week.

A woman walked by, her brows furrowed as she looked at the wall of products.

"Can I help you find something?" Dani asked.

The woman looked at her and shook her head. "Sorry, you're too young."

"Excuse me?"

"I want to talk to someone my age about products. You have great skin and you're young. You can't imagine what I need."

Dani smiled tightly. She'd heard that complaint from customers before. They assumed because she was only twenty-two that she didn't understand the needs of women older than her. "Actually, I handle all my mom's skincare and makeup needs. You look like you're younger than her, so I'm sure I'd be able to help you. I understand if you don't trust me because of my age, but I promise I won't lead you astray."

The woman's eyes narrowed slightly and then she said, "All right. But don't recommend anything too crazy. No pink eye shadow or weird-colored lipstick."

"I promise."

By the time the store closed at nine, Dani's feet were aching. Her shoes were cute, but they did a number on her toes. "Any plans for the weekend?" Dani asked Freida, the store's manager.

"Going to my mother-in-law's Saturday to watch my hubby and his brother install a shower in her bathroom. So you know, I'm living the dream."

Dani grinned. "Sounds like it."

"You?"

"Nothing as far as I know. My mom said she wanted to do something, but my dad and brother are working on a big build and trying to get it finished on time, so I don't know if we'll actually do anything or not."

"They're building something for the zoo, right?"

"The safari park, yeah."

"Cool. I haven't been there since I was a kid."

"Me either. Maybe I'll volunteer to help them out. Or I might just decide to pamper myself and sleep in."

"Now that I'd love to do. The older I get the more I realize how great naps are."

Dani said goodnight to Freida and walked to her car. She sat behind the wheel and texted her mom that she was on the way home, then found a playlist on her music app and waited for it to load. Once her favorite pop tunes were blaring through the speakers, she put the phone in the cup holder and buckled up, heading for home.

Beauty was a twenty-five-minute drive from where Dani had grown up and still lived, in the town of Little River. There wasn't much in Little River–a gas station with a mini-mart that served the best sandwiches on the planet and a campsite where people could rent kayaks and canoes in the summer.

She liked the quietness of the town, but she also got tired of it. There wasn't anything to do in Little River, and there definitely weren't any guys she could date who she hadn't already dated. Her father's construction business employed four other men who were all in their twenties–Crew, Avi, Grey, and Ford–but while she found them good-looking, her father had forbidden her from dating any of them. It hadn't mattered in the long run, because they all treated her like a little sister anyway, and she thought of them as big brothers. The last thing on her mind when she was around them was dating.

She parked on the street in front of the two-story colonial and turned off the engine. Her father's truck was in the driveway, as was her mom's sedan. Khyle, her brother, didn't live at home anymore. He and the guys lived in an apartment complex fifteen minutes away. Dani wanted to move out, but she couldn't afford to make rent on her own. She didn't mind living at home, though. At least not right now, anyway. She didn't have to worry about rent or utilities, and her mom was a great cook.

Dani got out of the car and walked up the sidewalk, finding the front door unlocked which told her that her parents were still up. She heard the television and smiled as she made her way to the family room. Her mom was curled up on the couch, a book in her lap and her reading glasses perched on her nose, and her dad was in his favorite recliner, watching a police show.

"Hey sweetie," her dad, Dexter, said.

"Hi."

"How was work?" her mom, Nancy, asked.

"Good. Long." Dani stepped out of her heels and wiggled her toes in the carpet. "I gave my card to a woman getting married in a few months. And I saw online that James Ray High School's homecoming is in a month, so I thought I could advertise my services for makeup on social media and target young people in that town and the surrounding areas."

"Pretty smart," Dexter said, smiling broadly.

"Well, Grey said that if I want to grow my business I can't just rely on word of mouth or hope that people needing a makeup artist would happen to come into Beauty."

"He's not wrong," Dexter said.

"When do you work next?" Nancy asked.

"I open on Monday, so I have the weekend off." She looked at her father. "Could you use a hand tomorrow?"

His brows rose. "You'd like to help out on the job site on your day off?"

She shrugged. "I could use some extra cash to refill my supplies and pay for online marketing."

"I could definitely use a hand with the clean-up. We're getting ready for the flooring guys, so everything has to be cleaned."

"I'm game. It comes with lunch, right?" she asked.

He laughed. "Of course. I'm leaving at seven."

"I'll be up."

She said good night to her parents and headed up to her bedroom on the second floor. As she got ready for bed, her mind strayed to the thought that had been crossing her mind a lot recently–her forever guy. She knew her Mr. Right was out there somewhere. She just had to find him.

Wherever he was.

Dani yawned, her jaw cracking with the motion, and then took a drink of coffee.

"You slept well?" her dad asked. He glanced at her then returned his gaze to the road.

"Yep. Well, I tossed and turned a bit. I had some weird dreams. Or one weird dream broken up by periods of wakefulness."

"Oh? What about?"

"I was at a wedding. It was mine, but I couldn't see who I was marrying. I kept trying to get down the aisle, but there were people blocking my path."

He hummed. "That's interesting."

"I've been thinking a lot about finding Mr. Right."

There was a beat of silence, and then he said, "Since when?"

"The last month or so, maybe? I don't know. It's like all of a sudden, I randomly think about what my future will look like, when I'll meet my forever guy. Maybe it's just because I haven't been on a date in six months."

He got quiet again. She gave him a sidelong glance and saw his brow was furrowed. She was about to ask him if everything was okay, when he cleared his throat and said, "Do you believe in fate?"

She blinked in surprise. "You mean romantically, right?"

He nodded, not taking his eyes off the road.

"Yeah, I do. I love the idea of knowing your soulmate on sight. It's just... pretty damn cool."

"Soulmate?"

"You don't like that word or something?"

"Usually you say Mr. Right. I've just never heard you say soulmate."

"Well, you and Mom say you're soulmates."

"True."

"It's not a bad word, is it? It's just another way of saying Mr. Right."

He hummed. "Yes and no. I was actually brought up to believe that Mr. Right—or in my case Mrs. Right—was just a romantic notion created by the greeting card companies. But a soulmate is special. It's like love at first sight on steroids. The moment I saw your mom, honey, I knew she was meant to be mine. I'd have done anything to be with her."

Dani smiled at him. Dexter wasn't her biological father, who'd died from an accident in the military when she was a baby. Dexter had come into her and her mom's life when Dani was two. He'd married her mom and adopted Dani. His son, Khyle, was her step-brother, but they didn't talk about each other that way. Dexter and Khyle were her family—she'd never known anything but them. That Dexter had loved her mom at first sight made Dani so happy.

She wanted that.

"I'm glad you found Mom."

"Me, too." He cleared his throat. "I've been meaning to tell you that Monday night we're hosting a party at the house."

"Fun. What kind of party?"

"Just a casual thing. Some old friends of mine are coming in for a visit. We're putting them up in the bed and breakfast in Meyersville."

"I'm working Monday, but I'm off at four. I assume I'm invited since it's at our house?"

He smiled. "Of course. They'll be over around seven. It's just casual."

"You said that already."

"Said what?"

"That it was casual."

"Sorry, distracted by the road. So you'll come?"

"I'd never turn down a party invite."

He gave her a smile and hit the blinker, turning down the road that led to the new build. The park had hired her dad's company to build a small apartment complex at the back of the property. There were coded gates and high fences, ensuring the public couldn't access the apartments.

When he parked, she got out of the truck and stretched, looking around. "Why do they need apartments, anyway?"

"They said that at one point, a couple of their staff were looking for someplace to live, and so they'd converted a barn into three small apartments. They outgrew that building and hired us to build a larger complex."

"It's like the apartment complex at the boardwalk," she mused. One summer, she'd taken a job working a kiddie ride at the boardwalk, and she'd been offered one of the apartments nearby. She might have been willing to take them up on the offer, but she would've had to share the two-bedroom apartment with three other women, and she hadn't wanted to do that.

"Exactly. We're about a month out from finishing."

Khyle and the other four jogged over to them. "Morning," Khyle said.

Dexter clapped his hands together. "Dani's going to be cleaning starting on the second floor. Grey, you show her the ropes. The rest of you have your assignments. Joss is coming by later today to check progress."

"Who's Joss?" Dani asked as she followed Grey to the second floor of the small complex. They moved along the open walkway to the farthest apartment. He unlocked the front door and held it open for her, switching on the overhead lights.

"He's head of the finance department for the park," Grey said. "He's overseeing the project."

Grey showed her the ropes, which involved sweeping and mopping each room and wiping down the windows and baseboards. They'd already painted several of the apartments in preparation for the flooring company to come in later in the week.

"These are pretty nice apartments," she said as she took a bucket and filled it up with water. She carried it into the family room and dunked a sponge into it, wringing it out.

"Don't get any ideas," Grey said as he walked to the door.

"Ideas about what?" she asked.

"Trying to work here. Dex wouldn't like it."

She looked at him in confusion. "I'm not trying to work at the park, I was just saying they're nice apartments."

He narrowed his eyes. "I'm just saying, this isn't a place where Dex–or any of us–would want you hanging out. We're here for this job, and that's all."

Dani rolled her eyes at his big-brother attitude. "Calm down. Unless they're hiring a makeup artist for their zookeepers, I'm not interested."

Grey chuckled. "Just checking." He turned to leave and then glanced back at her. "Did Dex tell you about the party on Monday?"

"Yep."

"You're going to be there, right?"

"Yeah. Why?"

"Because it'll be good for you to meet some new people."

"I meet new people all the time at Beauty."

14

"Not men."

She hummed. "True. You're acting weird, by the way."

"Just looking out for you."

He disappeared, and she stared at the empty doorway. Had everyone in her life suddenly gone insane? Shaking her head, she turned her attention to the task at hand and got to work.

~

"Oh! Hi." A feminine voice startled Dani. She jerked in surprise and banged her head on the bathroom counter.

"Ouch, crap." Dani rubbed the side of her head and sat back on her heels.

A woman wearing a red golf shirt with the park's logo on it smiled at her from the open door. "Are you okay? I didn't mean to startle you."

"I'm fine," Dani said as she pushed up from the floor and wiped her hands on her jeans to dry them.

The woman extended her hand and Dani shook it. "I'm Jeanie. My husband, Joss, is overseeing the complex for the park. I came to take a peek around and heard someone in here."

"I'm Dani, Dexter's daughter."

"It's nice to meet you." Jeanie looked around the bathroom and smiled. "Do you like working for your father's company?"

"I don't really work for him; I'm just helping out. I work at Beauty."

"What's that?"

"It's a beauty supply store. We sell makeup, skin and hair care products, and beauty tools."

"Oh, neat. What do you do there?"

"I do makeovers and demo beauty products."

"Really? I have to confess I don't do much in the way of makeup. I'm a cook here at the park. I work in the employee cafeteria."

Dani smiled. So many women told her similar things about not using makeup. "I've always loved makeup. I went to cosmetology school."

"That's pretty neat. Do you do makeup for weddings and stuff?"

"Yeah. Not as much as I'd like to. I have a side business. I'd love to grow it, so I don't have to work as much at the store, but it's slow going."

"Do you have a business card? I might know some women who need help in that area."

Dani's heart pounded in excitement as she pulled her cell phone from her back pocket and pulled a card from the wallet stuck to the back of the sparkly pink case. "Here you go. I'd love any referrals you can give me, and I'd even be happy to do some makeup for you too in exchange for them."

Jeanie stared at the card for a long moment and then took out a rectangular piece of colorful paper from her pocket. "We brought some tickets for the VIP safari tours for your dad and his workers, but they said they weren't interested. Would you like one?"

Dani accepted the ticket. "Wow, that would be awesome. I've never been on a safari tour."

"These are a little different," Jeanie said. "This ticket gets you free parking and admittance into the park. You just have to go online and reserve your spot–tours are Fridays through Sundays year-round. It's a private tour; just you, a driver, and a guide."

"I'd love to check it out," Dani said. She followed Jeanie into the family room.

"Check what out?" Khyle asked as he stood in the doorway with a man Dani thought was probably Joss, judging by the way he pulled Jeanie into his arms and smiled at her like he couldn't quite breathe right when she wasn't around.

"The VIP tour." Dani showed him the ticket.

Khyle narrowed his gaze. He turned to Joss. "If there's nothing else?" he said, his tone clipped and dismissive.

Joss glanced between Khyle and Dani. "No, we're done here."

"It was nice to meet you, Dani," Jeanie said.

"You, too."

When the couple left, Khyle snatched the ticket from Dani's hand and tore it up.

"Hey!" she said. "What the hell did you do that for?"

Dexter strode into the apartment. "What's going on?"

"They fucking gave Dani a ticket after we said no."

Dexter grunted, and it sounded a lot like a growl. He looked over his shoulder out the open door, a deep frown on his face. When he turned back to Dani, he said, "You can't go on the tour."

"Why not? It's just a fun thing to do."

"Because it's not appropriate. I'm your father, and I know what's best for you."

Dani opened her mouth to argue that she was an adult and could certainly go on a safari tour if she wanted to, but the look on her dad's face told her arguing wasn't going to do any good. Once more, she thought the men in her life were acting odd. First her dad, then Grey, and now Khyle. What the hell was going on?

"Fine, I won't," Dani said. "Khyle tore up the ticket anyway."

"Just so we're on the same page," Dexter said. "You're here to help us out, not venture into the park. Got it?"

Nodding, she turned to go back into the bathroom to finish wiping the baseboards. Khyle grabbed her arm. "Don't be mad, D. We just know some things that you don't, and you need to trust us."

"I do trust you. You just don't have to be so damned heavy-handed with me. Tearing up the ticket was a little over the top."

He tucked the ripped ticket into his pocket. "I'm feeling dramatic today."

"Obviously."

"We're cool?" he asked, giving her a lopsided smile.

"Yep."

"Good. See you at lunch break."

She returned to the bathroom, disappointed. She'd really liked the idea of going on the tour, even if she'd only had the ticket in her hand for a few minutes. She couldn't believe her brother tore the thing up.

As she got to work, she tried to put the safari tour out of her mind, but she couldn't shake the idea that it was important. That her being here on this day, talking to Jeanie, and getting the ticket were all part of some big master plan for her life. What if going on the tour gave her an opportunity to get some work for her business?

Her phone buzzed, and she dropped the sponge into the bucket with an irritated sigh. Wiping her hand off, she looked at the screen then answered the call.

"Hi, it's Jeanie. I was wondering if you had time tonight for a makeup job? My husband just asked me out on a date, and I'd love to look really nice for him."

Dani grinned. "What time? I'll have to run home and grab my supplies. We're here until five."

"Would seven-thirty work?"

"Sounds perfect. Where should I meet you?"

"You can use the parking pass with the VIP coupon, I'll just let them know at the gate."

Dani winced. "The ticket got ruined. I don't have it anymore."

"Oh! Well, I'll leave your name at the gate and meet you at the entrance."

"See you then!"

Dani smiled and put the phone back in her pocket. She had a job! And maybe she could ask Jeanie for another VIP tour ticket. And this time, she'd keep it to herself and not let her family know what she was doing.

They were definitely hiding something from her. She wondered if it had to do with the party on Monday.

Whatever their reasons were, it didn't really matter to her. She wanted to do the tour, and she'd find a way to do it.

CHAPTER THREE

Dani hustled into the house and straight up to her bedroom, shutting the door and stripping as she walked to her bathroom. She was exhausted from working for ten hours scrubbing the apartments. Despite the aches, she was thrilled to go back to the park and help Jeanie.

The hot water from the shower felt heavenly on her skin. She twisted the showerhead to the pulse and turned away from the spray, letting the heat pepper her neck and shoulders. Rolling her head, she stretched and sighed, letting the kinks get worked out of her joints.

She dressed in a pair of black pants and a black three-quarter sleeve top. A small heart pendant and her favorite woven bracelet were all the jewelry she wore. After fixing her long dark hair into a bun, she applied makeup–concealer to cover the dark circles that a day of hard work had given her, mascara to bring out her eyes, and a bit of pink lip gloss.

Smiling at her reflection, she grabbed her supplies stowed in a train case and a small leather duffel, and headed downstairs.

"Where are you off to?" her mom asked as Dani stopped in the kitchen and filled up a water bottle.

"I took a client," she said. Twisting the lid closed on the ice water, Dani kissed her mom on the cheek. "I won't be too late."

"Oh. Well, your dad wanted to talk to you. Can you wait a few minutes until he's out of the shower?"

No, Dani thought, she couldn't. Because she didn't want him to ask too many questions. She was twenty-two, but sometimes her dad made her feel about ten years old.

"Tell him to text me, I gotta jam. Love you!"

Dani walked quickly from the house, her bags jostling against her shoulder as she hurried to her car. Once she was on the way, she relaxed, glad she hadn't been stopped. She wasn't one to lie to anyone, particularly her parents. She cherished honesty. But something was going on with her dad–and her brother and his friends–and she hadn't been able to shake the thought all day.

It wasn't just the party on Monday or the torn-up ticket or the conversation about soulmates.

She felt like she'd been suddenly cut out of a conversation by the people she loved.

As she drove to the park, her thoughts circled back to the dream she'd told her dad about. She wondered why he'd cared about it, but he'd seemed interested. It was just a dream, of course. She never put much stock in dreams. But it had felt very real, like a vision of her future. She might have thought she had weddings on the brain because of her business, but if that were the case, then wouldn't she always dream of weddings?

Deciding she'd think more about it later, she focused on the road and turned up the volume when one of her favorite tunes began. Singing at the top of her lungs, she drove to the

Amazing Adventures Safari Park, feeling hopeful and excited.

~

"There," Dani said, holding up a mirror for Jeanie to look in. "What do you think?"

"Oh, holy crap, you took off ten years!" Jeanie grinned, her eyes crinkling at the corners. "I look amazing. If I do say so myself."

Dani smiled. "You sure do."

Outside of the small office within the security building in the center of the park, Dani had set up a makeup station and done Jeanie's makeup. The woman was wearing a denim skirt and a cold-shoulder top.

"Do you think your husband will approve?"

Jeanie glanced at the door, where Joss was waiting just beyond it. "Definitely. I might not even make it to our date."

Dani giggled. "Thanks for letting me do your makeup." She began to put away her supplies.

"What do I owe you?"

"Nothing," Dani said. "You said you'd let your friends and coworkers know about me, and that's enough."

"No, no way. Let me at least pay for your gas."

"You don't have to. I really enjoyed it. I love doing makeup."

"I can tell," Jeanie said. "You were smiling the whole time."

"I'm lucky to be able to do what I want. I wish I could do it full time."

Jeanie stood and said, "What happened to the VIP ticket I gave you?"

"My brother didn't want me to use it. He took it from me."

"That's weird, why wouldn't he want you to have a free tour?"

"I have no idea."

"Well, here's another ticket," Jeanie said. "Unless you think you shouldn't take it? I don't want to cause a problem between you and your family."

"I'd love it, thank you. I really want to go on the tour. I kind of feel like... well, never mind."

"Feel like what?"

"Like I'm supposed to be here. I don't want you to think I'm crazy, though. It's just a feeling."

"I understand. You know, you can schedule the tour right here for tomorrow. I'm sure we've got some spots open."

"That would be great."

Jeanie helped Dani schedule a tour for three p.m. When she opened the door to the office, Joss smiled at her. "Wow, babe, you look amazing! Then again, I think you look amazing all the time."

He pulled her into his arms and twisted away from the center of the room, pushing his wife against the wall. He said something low, and Jeanie giggled. She leaned around Dani and said, "I told you he was going to want to stay home."

"I'm glad it's got his approval."

"Come on," Jeanie said, "we've gotta walk Dani to her car. Then you can take me out. I promise it'll be worth the wait."

"I love how you think," Joss said.

Joss, Jeanie, and two other men walked Dani out of the park and to her car. She accepted a hug from Jeanie. "Thanks again," Jeanie said.

Dani opened the door and said, "Anytime."

"Good luck tomorrow," Jeanie said.

Dani frowned. "Why would I need luck on the tour?"

Jeanie shrugged, a small smile curving the side of her lips. "I mean, have fun."

"I will. You, too."

Dani sat behind the wheel and turned on the engine, closing her door and waving at the small group. She backed out of the spot and headed for home, a tune in her heart and the tour on her mind.

Neo lunged for the bottom branch of a tree and swung himself up into the canopy. He turned and leaned against the trunk, wiggling to scratch an itch between his shoulder blades. He settled on the wide branch and looked through the leaves at the Jeep and the human female who was standing at the fence, talking to Jasper, one of the wolf tour guides.

The female was pretty, but not Neo's soulmate.

The Jeep moved on, and Neo let out a deep sigh. It was the last tour of the day. Because it was fall, the sun set earlier, which meant that the tours didn't stay open as late as they did in the summer.

Below, Atticus grunted up at him, his dark eyes questioning.

It would be handy if they could talk in their shifts, but that wasn't possible. He knew, though, that Atticus was asking if he was okay.

Nodding, Neo let his head fall back against the trunk and stared up to the darkening sky. He rubbed the space over his heart as he thought about the VIP tours and the unmated females who had come through the park that day. He'd been in his shift since two p.m. and had seen ten females. None of them were a soulmate for him or any of the other gorillas. If one of them had been a soulmate for another shifter group, they'd have heard the good news by now.

That it was just another day at the park meant the tours

had failed once more to bring a soulmate for someone. Anyone.

Neo wanted it to be him. He wanted to call dibs like a teenager and beg whoever was in charge of soulmates in the universe to please, please bring him his female.

But he couldn't call dibs. It was ridiculous to even consider.

The sun set fully, and Neo swung down from the tree and landed on the ground. Adriana, wearing a zookeeper uniform, was holding a bunch of bananas. Neo took the one she offered him, and sat a few feet away and ate it, wondering if the tours were a good idea or not. So far, only four soulmates had come through the VIP tours–Adriana, Celeste, Harmony, who had bought her own ticket, and Jeanie who had used her neighbor's ticket.

Alfie, one of the wolves who patrolled the tour area, came to the fence. "It's all clear, guys."

That was their signal that all the humans were gone from the area and it was safe to shift. Neo headed toward the shed in the center of their paddock. Once inside, he shifted back to human and grabbed his clothes from the table. It was after eight, and he was starving.

"Wanna grab a beer?" August asked as he pulled his shirt over his head.

Neo fastened his jeans. "I think I'm going to get something to eat in the park."

"The park? Why?" August asked.

"I don't know. I feel like being topside."

"The local bar is topside," August pointed out.

Neo smiled at his friend. "Yeah. I'm not in the mood for a beer."

"Okay, maybe tomorrow."

Neo headed for the door, and Atticus grabbed his arm. "You sure you're okay?"

"Yep."

Atticus eyed him and then said, "If you need to talk, I'm here."

"I know, thanks."

Neo jogged across the paddock and opened the man-sized door at the side of the fence, closing and locking it behind him. He followed the trail, making his way into the heart of the park where the food stalls were manned by bear shifters. He inhaled, sorting through the scents and trying to decide what he wanted to eat.

And then he smelled something amazing.

He followed the scent to the security office. Opening the door, he stepped inside.

"Hey, Neo," Lucius, one of the lions, said from behind the counter.

"Was... do you smell that?" Neo asked.

Lucius inhaled. "I don't smell anything but makeup."

"Makeup?"

"Yeah, Joss's mate was in here getting a makeover from a human female. They just left about ten minutes ago."

Neo's heart clenched as he inhaled a second time. He picked up the scent of some kind of powder, which he thought might be makeup. But underneath that was a sweet scent that called to his gorilla.

"Do you know where they went?" Neo asked.

"Whoa, are you okay? Your eyes are brown." Lucius frowned.

Shaking his head and pushing back on his beast, Neo said, "I think the human is my soulmate."

CHAPTER FOUR

Neo paced in the security office, waiting for Joss to respond to Lucius's text. Neo had raced out into the parking lot to see if he could find Joss but had been unable to locate him. The female's scent that had captivated him had dispersed in the wide-open space, carried away on the breeze. He'd returned to the security office and waited for Joss's call.

Which seemed to be taking forever.

Lucius's phone finally buzzed, and he put it on speaker.

"Hey, Joss, it's Lucius."

"I'm on a date with my soulmate." Joss's tone was clipped and annoyed, but Neo didn't care who he insulted.

"I followed a scent into the security office. I believe it belongs to my soulmate," Neo said.

There was a beat of silence and then Joss said, "Who is this?"

Neo ground his teeth together to stop from roaring in frustration. "It's Neo."

Joss hummed. "The female is human. She came to the

park to help Jeanie with her makeup for our date tonight. Which, if you missed it earlier, is where we are. On a date."

"I understand," Neo said, failing to hide his displeasure. Was the alpha not going to help him?

"Neo, it's Jeanie," she said. "Her name is Dani Fitzgerald. Her dad is the owner of the construction company doing the work on the apartment complex."

"You have a number where I can reach her?"

"No," Joss cut in. "She doesn't."

There was a short, muffled argument, and Jeanie said, "Sorry, Neo. Joss won't let me give you her number."

"Why the hell not?" Neo demanded. "I said she's my soulmate."

"She's human," Joss said, his voice dropping to a low growl. "And don't forget who you're talking to."

Neo wanted to punch something. How the hell unfair was this?

Jeanie cut in. "Neo, it's okay, I promise. The reason Joss won't give you her information is that we got the impression from Dexter that he didn't want her in the park. I gave her a VIP tour ticket, and she told me her brother took it from her. I gave her another one, and she scheduled a tour tomorrow at three."

He was puzzled. "Why don't they want her here?"

"No clue," Joss said. "But it's important that we don't do anything to screw up the relationship between us and them, since they're not done with the complex. If Dexter gets pissed and bails because Jeanie gave out his daughter's number, then we're going to be screwed."

"But hey, she's coming tomorrow," Jeanie cut in. "It's less than twenty-four hours from now. You can manage, right?" Jeanie asked.

Neo's gorilla hooted in annoyance. "Yes," he said, tightly.

"We'll be back in a few hours," Joss said. "I don't want to be disturbed again unless it's an emergency, and while your situation is pressing, it's certainly not worth me bringing my mate back to the zoo when we're not going to give you Dani's contact information anyway. Are we clear?"

Neo inhaled deeply and let it out slowly before answering. "I understand. Enjoy your date."

Joss grunted and disconnected the call. Neo stared at the phone, wishing he'd been ten minutes earlier topside. That he'd listened to his beast and gotten out of the paddock faster. He'd known something was going on, but he hadn't been certain, and it never crossed his mind that his soulmate might be somewhere in the park.

Lucius gave him a curious look. "You really think she's yours?"

Neo nodded. "Do you know anything about her? Did you talk to her?"

He shook his head. "Nah. I came in to relieve Jupiter, and I asked what the girly smells were. He told me about the human. Sounds like you just missed her."

Neo let out a sighing grunt. "I could kick my own ass."

"You'll see her tomorrow, though. Maybe you can work something out with the tour driver or guide and spend time with her."

His gorilla perked up. "You think?"

Lucius shrugged. "Joss took Jeanie on her tour by himself. I don't see why they wouldn't let you. You just have to clear it with Joss."

"I guess it's a good thing I didn't piss him off," Neo said.

"That's one male you don't want to mess with, that's for damn sure."

The following morning, Neo found Atticus in the market-place picking up a cord for his cell from Anke who ran a little shop with her mate, Zeger. Inside was everything from socks to electronics, and what they didn't have in stock, they would order.

"Hey, I've got some great news," Neo said.

"I heard," Atticus said. He took the cord from Anke and thanked her.

"You heard? How?"

Atticus jerked his head, and Neo followed him to an empty table. "Joss called."

"And?"

"He wanted to talk to me about the protocol for later today."

"I was going to ask if I could replace one of the wolves in the Jeep for Dani's tour, so I can spend time with her."

Atticus shook his head. "Joss and I both agreed that you need to be in your shift."

"What? Why?" Neo demanded.

Atticus's brow arched, and Neo cracked his neck and tried to settle his beast.

"Because you're more in tune with your nature in your shift. While neither of us think you're wrong and this female is likely your soulmate, the appropriate place for you to be isn't in the Jeep with her while you're human, but in the paddock in your shift. That way you'll know for sure she's yours, and we can handle it the way we're supposed to."

"I don't want to be trapped in my shift. What if she won't stick around?" Once he shifted, he'd be stuck for several hours until he could return to his human form.

"You can shift ahead of time," Atticus said. "Instead of waiting until two like the rest of us, you can go into the paddock early, which will allow you to return to human once her Jeep passes by. Assuming that she actually is your soulmate."

Neo opened his mouth to protest, but Atticus put up his hand.

"I know you're not happy, but remember that we've got protocols in place for this situation. She'll go on the tour, and your beast will let you know if she really is your soulmate. If so, you can hustle into the shed, shift and get dressed, and wait for her in the security office. A couple of wolves will bring her to the office so she can wait for her photo album and you can introduce yourself to her."

Neo's mind spun. "Could I take her out of the office? Like offer her a tour of the park?"

His alpha nodded. "That's exactly what I was thinking. Just remember that if you leave the park with her, you can't stay out overnight."

"I know."

Win, one of the gorillas, had permanently screwed every shifter's ability to spend the night away from the park after he'd fallen asleep at his soulmate's place and shifted while he slept. Scared the crap out of her and could've revealed their secret to the general human population, which wouldn't have been good. So now, no one could be away from the park overnight.

Unless their soulmate knew the truth of their shift and there wasn't any danger of anyone revealing anything they shouldn't.

"I don't know how to do this," Neo confessed, slumping back in the chair. "I don't know how to make her mine."

Atticus smiled knowingly. "First things first–make sure she's yours. Then the rest will work itself out."

"I'm sure she's mine."

"I'm happy for you," Atticus said. "Even though she didn't

get a VIP ticket in the mail, it still technically means you'll meet her on the tour, and that'll be a good morale boost for everyone."

"It's going to be a long wait," Neo said.

"You're only twenty-six," Atticus pointed out. "Talk to me when you're forty-seven."

"Sorry, sorry," Neo said. "You're right. I think I'm going to go to the maintenance shed."

"Oh?"

"I'm going to try to bury myself in work and make the time fly faster."

"Good luck with that."

Neo left the marketplace, stopping in his home to change into coveralls before making his way to the maintenance shed. He wasn't sure he'd be able to concentrate on anything except Dani, but he had to do something. If he sat home and did nothing, the time would drag. Setting his mind on the list of projects on the tablet, he selected the most pressing and got to work.

Afternoon couldn't come fast enough.

Dani felt the weight of the paper ticket in her pocket as she headed to her car Sunday afternoon. It was just a little piece of paper, but she couldn't help but feel like it weighed far more than that. Like it was significant in some way.

Like the rest of her life might start today.

It was a warm day, the sky a pretty blue and dotted with clouds, the breeze blowing and making the trees rustle. She'd been unable to sleep well the night before. She'd had some dreams, disjointed and odd, but she couldn't really remember them once she woke. She was troubled, but she was sure it was because she'd planned to go on the tour despite her family's insistence to the contrary.

It bothered her that Khyle had torn up the first ticket and that all six men in her dad's company–including her dad–had told her the park wasn't a place for her. She didn't see the harm in going to the park or taking advantage of Jeanie's kindness and going on the VIP tour. Dani had looked at the website during one of the times she'd awoken overnight and thought the tour looked like a lot of fun. She loved animals, even though she'd never been able to have a pet. Her mom had allergies and her dad wasn't a fan of pets in the house. The closest she ever came to having a real pet was a goldfish she'd had in elementary school.

Her dad loved horses and took her often to a farm down the road from their house, so she could watch them trot around the enclosure and take carrots and apples from her hand. She'd asked if they could have a horse when she was little, and he'd said that the farm down the road was close enough, so they didn't need a horse of their own.

She couldn't decide which of the animals on the safari tour she'd like the best. She was a fan of wolves, but also of lions. There was something neat about gorillas, though. And she was looking forward to seeing Tank, the grumpy moose that was the unofficial park mascot. She'd also read some online reviews that said the ice cream stall was well worth waiting in line for, with an "ice cream of the day" that was sure to be unique and delicious.

The drive to the park was uneventful, but she'd expected it to be. Or, rather, she'd hoped it would be, and that her dad or brother wouldn't pull some crazy driving moves and try to block her from getting to the park.

When she'd left the house, they were getting the food ready for the Monday night party. She didn't miss how her family stopped talking when she walked into the kitchen to say goodbye. She had no idea what they were discussing, but she couldn't shake the feeling that she was the topic.

Pulling into line behind a few other vehicles, she waited her turn to go through the gate into the parking lot.

"Hi," she said, greeting the man in the booth.

He scanned the VIP tour ticket then handed it back to her. "Follow the signs to the VIP parking area, then hand your ticket to the person at the gate, and they'll direct you from there. Have fun!"

She set the ticket on the seat and thanked him, pulling forward and following the signs. She parked and grabbed her ticket and crossbody bag, then got out of the car. It was a gorgeous fall day. She'd dressed casually in jeans and hiking boots, with a short-sleeved shirt and light jacket. Putting her bag over her shoulder, she headed toward the entrance to the park, then through a huge set of wrought iron gates with animal silhouettes in the center of each one.

After her bag was checked and she walked through a metal detector, she was given a map and directed to the safari tour check-in. There were a few people in line ahead of her. She leaned against the rail and looked at her phone for the first time since she'd left home.

She had several text messages. One from her brother, asking if she wanted to see a movie with him and the guys, one from her mom asking if she'd be home for dinner, and one from her dad asking where she was.

The line moved forward one person as a blue camouflage-painted Jeep pulled up and a man escorted the first-in-line woman to it.

Dani answered two of the texts but couldn't decide how she wanted to answer her dad. If she told him she'd come to the park against his wishes, he'd be pissed, and she didn't like to disappoint him. But she was an adult, and she'd made a choice.

How could she explain to him that she'd felt compelled to come to the park and go on the safari tour? That the whole drive to the park had felt like it was leading to something important?

He believed in fate and love at first sight, but he'd think she was a lunatic if she told him she thought she was supposed to come to the park. She wasn't even sure she understood her own desire to be here herself.

"I don't want you to be disappointed," she typed to her dad, "but I'm at the park about to go on the safari tour. I feel like I need to do this. Hope you understand."

"Hi, are you Danielle?" a man asked.

She looked up from her phone, unaware that the two women in front of her had already gotten into Jeeps and disappeared. "Yep."

Not waiting for a reply to her text, she put her phone in her bag and shook the man's hand as he introduced himself. "I'm Greg."

"Nice to meet you," she said, following him to the waiting Jeep.

Two young men smiled at her as Greg introduced them.

The driver, Silvanus, welcomed her to the VIP tour. The guide, Felix, helped her into the back seat and then faced backward to talk to her.

"Have you ever been to the park before?" Felix asked.

"Not since I was a kid."

"We hear that a lot," he said.

"Hold on, Danielle, the Jeep lurches a bit," Silvanus said.

Dani held onto the seat in front of her, steadying herself as it jerked forward and moved to a tall gate that was slowly opening.

The first stop on the tour was the elephant paddock. The Jeep stopped in front of a tall chain-link fence. Beyond the links she could see elephants milling around.

Felix got out and offered her his hand. "I... I'm getting out?"

"Sure," he said. "I'm going to take your picture at each paddock for the souvenir album with all your photos you'll get after the tour's over. Free of charge, of course."

"Neat."

She got out and waited while he took a fancy-looking camera out of the bag and slung it over his neck. He rattled off a series of facts about elephants and then took her picture.

They returned to the Jeep, which started on its way to the next paddock. "The next one is our favorite," Felix said.

"Oh? Which one is that?"

Felix had an excited look in his eyes, and she gave him a smile. He was cute. Not take-him-home-to-mom cute, but not bad looking at all.

"The wolves."

"Ah. Any reason?" she asked.

Felix cast a side glance at Silvanus who was grinning. "We just like them. Wolves rule, you know."

She laughed. "I didn't, but that's good to know."

Once they'd stopped in front of the next paddock, Felix helped her out of the Jeep and walked with her to the fence. The wolves noticed their approach and began to move toward them. Craning her neck, she looked at the top of the fence and then dropped her head to look at the wolves.

"Do they have names?"

"Sure," he said. "See that one with the white feet? That's Benjamin. And the one next to him is Thomas."

"Who decides the names?"

Felix frowned and then said, "The zookeepers."

"That would be a fun job."

"Naming wolves or being a zookeeper?"

"The naming thing. I don't know if I'd want to be a zookeeper. Seems dangerous."

"Our animals are all really friendly."

"What about Tank?"

Felix grinned. "He's not dangerous, just grumpy."

After her picture was taken, Felix looked past her to the wolves, and she had a strange feeling that he was communicating with them in some way. Which seemed entirely odd and not at all likely.

She was going to ask him what he was doing, when he smiled brightly and said, "Ready for the next paddock?"

"Sure," she said.

He helped her into the vehicle and in moments they were driving slowly along the dirt trail, leaving the wolves behind. The next paddock contained lions. After her photo at the fence, Felix said, "Up next is the gorillas."

The Jeep moved slowly along the path and drew to a stop in front of another paddock. She couldn't explain it, but something was pulling her from the Jeep before Felix even got out. She climbed over the side and hopped down, brushing suddenly trembling hands down her jeans.

She looked through the fence at the handful of gorillas milling around and her eyes locked with one. He was a foot away from the fence, and he was staring right at her. A connection shot through her, like she was meant to be there, meant to see this gorilla.

Which sounded entirely absurd in her head.

Really, why would a girl be destined to meet a gorilla at a park?

She walked right up to the fence, drawn by some invisible thread, and hooked her fingers in the links. The other gorillas were watching them, their dark eyes on her.

That's when she noticed the gorilla didn't have dark eyes.

Or, rather, they'd been dark, but then they were blue. An oddly human blue.

The gorilla moved forward and rose onto his back legs, covering her hands with his own. He was much taller than her petite five-foot-three. He settled his fingers over her hands, the warm, calloused pads rubbing lightly.

"Your eyes," she whispered, mesmerized.

Some part of her thought she was crazy for being so close to such a huge beast. She knew he was strong and could probably rip through the fence if he wanted to. But she wasn't afraid.

He hooted softly, his eyes flashing from blue to brown and back to blue again.

"I think we should get on with the rest of the tour," Felix said.

She felt him come close and put his hand on her shoulder. The gorilla snarled, a deep growl rumbling in his chest. His gaze turned murderous, focused entirely on the man behind her.

Felix's hand jerked off her shoulder. "Sorry, Neo."

She didn't take her gaze from the gorilla as she spoke to the tour guide. "His name is Neo?"

"Yes."

"You just apologized to him."

"Yeah, I guess I did."

"It's pretty weird," she said, not taking her gaze from Neo's. "I feel like I was meant to be here."

"I think it's pretty clear that you were," Felix said. "We'll finish the tour and go to the security office to wait. Understand?"

She tilted her head and looked at Felix. "Are you talking to me or Neo?"

"Both," he said. Then he smiled. "I think it'll all make sense to you in a little while. Just trust me."

"Okay."

Neo moved his hands from hers, hooting softly. She felt reassured by the sounds, even though it seemed very surreal.

"Maybe I'll see you again someday," she said to him.

Sadness swept over her, and she had to remind herself that this was an animal and whatever strange connection she was feeling to him didn't really mean anything.

Right?

CHAPTER FIVE

Neo knew the moment that the Jeep Dani was riding in was on the way. Hell, he'd felt her come into the park. Something within his soul pinged like echolocation, and he was certain he could have found her right then if he'd been allowed to leave the paddock in his shift. Which he absolutely wasn't.

He hadn't been able to sleep the night before, and he'd been up before dawn, anxious for the hours to speed by so he could see Dani. While the consensus among their group was that he had in fact found his soulmate, he was frustrated that he hadn't been able to get her contact information earlier. He understood about protocols, and the need for their people to be sure Dani was his soulmate, but damn if he was irritated by the wait.

He'd been fine before he scented her. Now he felt like part of him was missing, aching.

Three Jeeps came by ahead of hers. He sat near the fence, scenting the air and watching for her. He had no idea what she looked like. Joss had told Jeanie to keep the details to herself because they didn't want to influence him.

He really thought they were going overboard with the secrecy thing.

In the end, he hadn't needed to know anything about her. His beast was one hundred percent attuned to her, from the moment she stepped foot in the park until the Jeep she was in stopped in front of their paddock.

Damn she was beautiful.

She looked like a goddess, with long dark hair and pretty hazel eyes. She was dressed casually in jeans and a top, and he liked the way the jeans clung to her, highlighting her curves. She came right up to the fence, never breaking eye contact with him.

He could feel his beast wanting to let go and shift into his human form. He struggled mentally with keeping a tight leash on the beast, who wavered between wanting to shift and wanting to rip the fence apart to hold her. He didn't scent any fear from her, only curiosity.

She'd mentioned his eyes, and he knew it was because he was having a hard time holding onto his beast. He could feel that his eyes were changing color because they ached a little every time his beast tried to shift back into human.

Then he'd wanted to rip Felix's hand off for touching her shoulder.

As the Jeep pulled away with his soulmate, he turned and raced toward the maintenance shed in the center of the paddock, his band hooting and slapping their palms on the ground in celebration.

Once inside the shed, he was so excited to see Dani that he had trouble shifting into his human form, which was ironic since he'd spent quite a while in front of Dani trying *not* to change forms. Once he'd settled down enough to be able to shift, he dressed in jeans and a golf shirt with the park logo on the breast pocket. He lifted the door hidden in the floor and hurried down the stairs. He'd made this trip hundreds of times but felt like this one took forever.

When he finally made it to the security office, he stepped inside and looked around.

Jupiter, one of the lions, said, "She's at the norm paddock right now."

Neo let out a sigh that was part relief that he hadn't missed her and part irritation that she wasn't in the office already. "Okay, thanks."

"I went through the same thing when I met Celeste," Jupiter said. "It's hell waiting for them. You can have a seat in the office."

"I think I'll just pace, if that's okay."

"Sure, I get it." He paused for a moment and then said, "The alphas asked me to make sure you understand the protocol."

"I do."

Jupiter leaned on the counter and gave him a long look.

Neo stopped pacing and blew out a breath, forcing himself to think clearly. "I can't share the secret nature of our people until I'm certain she's in love with me and won't tell anyone else about it. And I can't stay overnight with her outside of the park."

"Right, and you can't do anything that might arouse suspicion with her family, like try to move her into the park before the apartment complex is finished."

"I promise I won't do anything to jeopardize our people."

"Good." Jupiter's phone buzzed on the counter, and he looked at the screen. "All right, they're finished with the tour. Jasper is going to escort her here."

Jasper was one of the wolves who handled tickets at the Safari tour.

Neo paced by the windows. He could feel Dani drawing

closer to the office, and he watched out one of the windows until he saw her.

His beautiful soulmate.

Jasper opened the door to the office and let Dani in, but didn't follow her. "Neo, this is Dani. I told her you'd explain about the photo album."

"Thanks," Neo said.

Jasper smiled at him. "No problem. Nice to meet you, Dani."

She stared at Neo, her hazel eyes wide. "Yep."

Neo smiled. She looked as flustered as he felt.

Jasper gave Neo a thumbs-up and shut the office door. Neo was aware of Jupiter leaving the main room and going into one of the offices to give them privacy.

"Hi Dani," Neo said, extending his hand.

Her gaze slipped from his face to his hand. She grasped it, her fingers cold and her hand trembling. "Hi."

"Would you like to sit?"

"Sure."

Their hands still connected, they walked over to a row of padded chairs and sat. He turned slightly so he could face her, drinking in everything about her. She smelled amazing– sweet like vanilla and spicy like cinnamon. Her hair wasn't just brown, it was a mixture of shades from chocolate to caramel, hanging past her shoulders in glorious waves.

She bit her bottom lip and gave him a tentative smile.

"Did you enjoy the tour?" he asked.

"Yeah. It was fun. Weird, but fun."

"How was it weird?"

"Well..." She shook her head. "No, you'll think I'm crazy."

"I promise I won't."

"I really liked one of the animals. It was so strange. I felt like my whole life was leading up to the moment I met him. I..." She rose to her feet suddenly, her eyes wide. "Oh my gosh, your name is the same as the gorilla. Is this some kind of joke?"

He stood slowly. "It's not a joke, Dani. My name is Neo."

"So you and the gorilla have the same name? That doesn't make sense." She took a step away from him, her eyes darting toward the door.

He didn't like that she was scared. The smell made his beast crazy. "Dani, please–it's okay, I promise."

"Nothing about this is okay," she said. "Is that what you people do on the tours? Tell the VIP an animal's name and then have someone meet them with that same name? I should go."

The sound that came from his mouth was all gorilla.

She squeaked in alarm and took another step back.

"Dani, please," Neo said. "Don't be afraid of me."

"Everything okay out here?" Jupiter asked from the office doorway.

"It's fine," Neo said. "I was just about to take Dani on a tour of the park so we could talk."

"Dani?" Jupiter asked.

She swallowed audibly, and he could scent her fear subsiding. "I'm good, thanks."

Neo offered her his hand, and she shook her head. He dropped it and turned to open the door, allowing her to walk out ahead of him. She didn't bolt like a rabbit, so he took that as a good sign.

"I'm sorry you're upset and confused. There's nothing going on here except what appears to be a coincidence regarding my name and the gorilla's name."

"You're not trying to make a fool of me or anything?"

"I'd never do that."

Her eyes narrowed slightly, then she relaxed a fraction. "Okay. This has been a weird day. I just overreacted, I guess."

"It's okay, I promise. I've had some weird days myself, so I can understand. Are you hungry?"

"A little. I heard that there's an ice cream stall that's pretty awesome."

He hated to disappoint her. "Sorry. They're closed until spring."

"Oh, shoot. I was looking forward to that."

His mind spun, then he said, "There's some in the employee cafeteria. I could take you there."

"Really?"

"Sure."

Although he wanted to hold her hand, he refrained, and they walked together toward the employee cafeteria.

"So you work at the park?" she asked.

"Yep. I work on the park's vehicles in the maintenance department."

"Do you like it?"

"I do, actually. I heard from Jeanie that you're a makeup artist?"

"She told you?"

"Yeah, I was curious."

"But how did you know about me?"

She stopped walking and stared at him.

What the hell was he supposed to say? Not only were they in public around other humans, but he couldn't exactly tell her the truth–that his beast had scented her in the office and knew she was his soulmate. He unlocked the door to the employee cafeteria, glanced inside to see it was empty, and held the door for her.

Once they were inside, and anything he said wouldn't be picked up by human ears, he faced her. "I just had a feeling, you know? That there was someone in the park I was supposed to meet. I followed that feeling to the office and learned that you'd been there. I asked Jeanie for your number to call you, but her husband wouldn't give it to me. He said I could meet you today when you came on the tour."

Her brows rose. "You were waiting for me today?"

He nodded. "Do you ever feel like you were destined to meet someone, Dani? Like your whole life was leading up to one moment?"

She let out a soft sound, her brows drawing down. She opened her mouth, but then frowned as she looked behind him.

The door to the cafeteria opened, and Joss was standing in the doorway.

"Dani, your family is at the gate demanding we bring you to them," Joss said.

"What? Are you serious?" she asked.

"Very. Neo?" Joss said his name like a question, but he could feel that it was more of a demand. Joss expected Neo to comply, so he would, or he'd face some consequences from the alpha wolf.

His gorilla wanted him to face off against the wolf, but the male in him who deferred to the alpha knew that was as dangerous as it was foolish. Joss was alpha for a reason, and it wasn't because he'd won a popularity contest. And Atticus would never stand for Neo to disrespect another alpha.

Neo looked at Dani. "Sweetheart, I think you should go to your family."

"But I thought…" Her voice trailed off and Neo's heart cracked. He could practically taste her confusion and sense of betrayal.

"I'll give you my cell number," Neo said. "Then you can call me when you're ready to see me again."

She lifted her phone from her pocket and swiped her thumb across it. Her hands were trembling, so he took it and entered his information into a text and sent it to himself, so she'd have his number and he'd have hers. He kissed her cheek and put her phone in her hands. "This doesn't mean I don't want to see you or be with you, Dani," he murmured in her ear. "There's just things at play here that neither of us can ignore."

He leaned away, and she blinked luminous eyes at him. She looked like she was on the verge of tears, and his gorilla hooted in his mind at her distress. She let out a shuddering breath and clutched her phone. "You promise you feel like I do? Even if I can't put it into words just yet?"

"I swear on my life that I felt drawn to you and I know you feel the same. Whatever you need to deal with concerning your family—you do it and then come back to me. I'll be waiting."

She blinked rapidly, and a tear slipped down her cheek. He brushed it away with his thumb. "I'll be back."

"I know you will."

He took her hand and followed Joss out into the afternoon sunshine. The walk to the gate was quiet. He wanted to beg her not to leave, to tell her to ignore her family's wishes and stay with him, but that wasn't fair. Not only was he facing the displeasure of the wolf alpha, but he had a feeling that there was more going on here than an overprotective father.

He recognized Dexter, the owner of the construction company, and figured the male for her father. He couldn't recall the name of the male next to him, but assumed it was Dani's brother.

"Dad," she said, when she saw him.

"We'll speak at home," Dexter said.

Neo had the urge to drop to his knees and show his neck to the male, which made no sense. His gorilla would never show deference to anyone but an alpha, and Dexter was human. Wasn't he?

Neo scented the air discreetly but picked up nothing but human.

"I'll see you soon, Dani," Neo said, giving her hand a squeeze.

She gave him a watery smile, and he wanted to hug her tightly and say to hell with her family. He wanted to shift into his gorilla and pound his chest, daring her family to take his soulmate from him.

But he didn't.

He watched her walk away between her dad and brother, her shoulders hunched and the scent of her sorrow hanging in the air like wet rags.

"Damn that was tough, son, I'm sorry," Joss said.

Neo inhaled deeply and rolled his shoulders. "I'm pissed that she's so upset."

"We need to talk," he said. "In the conference room."

Neo nodded and headed to the underground conference room, his heart heavy and his gorilla railing at the unfairness of the situation. Dani was his soulmate and she should be by his side, not snatched away before they could really even talk.

Ignoring his beast's urge to race back into the parking lot and take her into his arms, he turned his attention to the conference room as he neared it, surprised to see all the alphas looking grave.

Something was very wrong.

CHAPTER SIX

Dani folded her arms and stared at the open car door. "I'm not going anywhere until you guys tell me what the hell is going on."

Her mother was seated in the passenger seat. "Language!"

"Mom, seriously? Dad and Khyle just fully embarrassed me and you're going to comment on my word choice?"

"Ladies don't curse."

Dani rolled her eyes and looked at her dad. "Talk to me."

"We'll talk at home," Dexter said, his knuckles turning white on the top of the door as he gripped it.

She looked toward the park, her heart panging.

"I don't want to leave."

"He let you go pretty quick, D," Khyle said. "I think that's saying something."

"Don't be an ass," she retorted. "He was clearly being respectful of Dad."

"Come on, honey," her mom said. "Let's go home."

"I can drive my own car home," she said.

"I'll drive it home," Khyle said, sticking out his hand. "Give me your keys."

She stared at his hand for a moment, feeling the pressure of her family and their expectations of her. With a sigh, she took her keys from her bag and dropped them in his hand. "This is not fair," she said as she sat down heavily in the backseat.

"It'll all make sense soon enough," Dexter said as he shut the door and got behind the wheel. "You have to trust us."

"I want to, but you're being unreasonable," she pointed out.

They left, Khyle falling into line behind them. Her mom tried to engage her in conversation, but Dani wasn't in the mood to chat. She wanted to go back to the park and find Neo. She'd never felt such a strong attraction to a guy before, and she just knew in her heart that he felt the same way about her. But the situation she now found herself in sucked.

Once they were home, she sat at the kitchen table with her parents and Khyle.

"We've got company coming tomorrow night," Dexter said, folding his hands on top of the table.

"I know."

"We just want you to meet them, honey," her mom said.

"I don't understand what any of this has to do with you tracking me down at the park and hauling me away like a kid who had a tantrum in a department store. I'm old enough to make my own romantic choices, and I choose Neo."

"No one is saying you're not an adult," her mom said. "There are things at work here that you don't understand, and we need you to trust us."

"Why should I trust you when you're obviously keeping things from me?"

"What do you mean?" Dexter asked.

"Like I haven't noticed that you stop talking whenever I walk into a room lately? And this party that you keep mentioning, I mean, what's up with that? It's never mattered before if I was around for one of your get-togethers, so why is this one so important?"

Dexter and Khyle shared a meaningful glance, and Dani wanted to scream at their tight-lipped behavior.

Slowly, her father faced her. She couldn't figure out what he was thinking because his look was inscrutable, but she was certain he wasn't going to budge.

"We'll explain everything when the time is right," Dexter said slowly as if he were measuring every word. "You might be old enough to make your own decisions, but your mother and I aren't asking for your trust, we're expecting it. Don't forget that we bought your car and phone, and we give you a roof over your head."

"Threats? That's nice," she said.

Her mom put a hand on Dexter's forearm and gave Dani a small smile. "Tomorrow night, everything will make sense."

"At the party," Dani said.

"Yes," Dexter said. "Until then, we're asking you to stay home and stay away from that male."

"I don't like this," she said.

"You don't have to like it, you just have to trust that we have your best interests at heart," Dexter said.

"Fine," she said. "I'll play along, but fair warning, I'm not happy. You never even asked me why I wanted to be with Neo."

"We'll ask you tomorrow night," Khyle said. He stood and pushed the chair in, the legs scraping against the tile floor. He kissed their mother, and asked Dexter to walk him out.

Before her dad left, he asked for her phone.

"Seriously?" Dani said.

"We said no contact, and that's what we meant," Dexter said.

"Let me guess, I'll get it back tomorrow night after the party." She pushed her phone across the table.

"Yes." Dexter turned off her phone and took it with him as he left to walk Khyle out.

"I'll ask, honey," her mom said.

"Ask what?"

"Why you want to be with him."

"I feel like we were supposed to meet. It was the craziest thing. There was even a gorilla there with his same name. I thought they were trying to prank me–like one of those reality shows, but it's just a coincidence. Still..." She let her words die off and stared out the window behind her mother to the backyard.

"Still what?" her mom prompted.

"I miss him. It feels crazy and right at the same time." She rubbed the space over her heart. "How can I like someone so much when I only spent a few minutes with him?"

Her mom didn't say anything, and Dani took her gaze from the window to look at her. "Mom?"

"Sorry, honey. I'm sorry you're in the middle of things right now, but it'll all be clear tomorrow. Now, I've got some more food prep to take care of. Do you want something to eat?"

"No, I'm good." Dani pushed away from the table and headed up to her bedroom.

When she'd shut her door, she flopped on the bed and stared at the ceiling. A few hours ago, she'd had freedom to do what she wanted. Now she was trapped. At least until tomorrow night. She couldn't fathom what the hell was so important about this party that she couldn't even text the sexy guy from the park. With his very kissable lips she hadn't even had a chance to try out.

Frustrated, she did the only thing she could think of–used her laptop to record and post a makeup tutorial. It wouldn't get Neo to her side, but it would make the time pass until she could get her phone back and get in touch with him.

≈

Neo stared open-mouthed at the alphas as they sat at the big table in the conference room.

"What did you just say?" he asked.

Atticus cleared his throat. "They're shifters."

"But Dani smells human. And her dad and brother do, too," Neo said.

"We know," Joss said. "We don't know what sort of shifters they are, but they're definitely like us. Whatever they are, they're either hiding the scent in some way or they naturally smell like humans so we can't discern that they're shifters."

"Fucking A," Neo said. He rubbed the space between his eyebrows with a groan. "When I met Dexter, I had the oddest urge to kneel before him and bare my throat. I thought it was strange, but if he's a shifter–an alpha–then that makes sense. My gorilla would never have that urge with a human, even the father of my soulmate. So what kind of shifters don't have a scent?"

"Obviously, we'd just be guessing," Caesar, the lion alpha, said. "They might be a prey shifter, but we really have no way of knowing until they confirm it."

"I think Dani felt connected to me. If she's a shifter, why wouldn't she have just come out and told me she was when we were alone in the office?"

Joss shrugged. "There are a lot of mysteries surrounding this situation, the least of which is whether we employed a shifter group to do the construction of our apartment complex without knowing."

"And if they know about us," Alistair, the elephant alpha, said, "why didn't they share what they are?"

The alphas all nodded in agreement.

"What am I supposed to do?" Neo asked.

"You have her information?" Atticus asked.

Neo nodded. "And she has mine."

"We think you should wait for her to contact you and see where things stand. We don't believe you charging after her like a deranged bull is going to accomplish anything except infuriate her family," Caesar said.

Joss nodded. "When she reaches out to you, be sure you're keeping Atticus updated so he can keep us in the loop."

"I will," Neo said. He dropped his head back and sighed. This was not how he thought the day might go.

"The important thing is that you found each other," Atticus said. "The rest will work itself out. Regardless of what her family believes about soulmates or our people, we have your back."

Neo lowered his head. "Thanks."

He pushed away from the table and stood. "I'm going to try to keep myself busy with work and hope she calls soon."

It was tempting to disregard the alphas' orders to let her contact him first, but he knew they were right. Neo had no idea what was going on with Dani and her family, and he didn't want to cause her problems. While it warred with him to be away from her, it wasn't like he knew her address and could go see her. She had to make the first move.

He hoped she'd make it soon.

"Honey, honey? Wake up." Dani startled awake with a gasp. "It's Mom, don't freak out."

"You scared me," Dani said, pressing a hand to her pounding heart. "What's going on?"

"I'm helping you get out of here so you can go to Neo."

"What?"

"Your dad is gone for a few hours." She held up her phone

and showed Dani a tracking app, the red dot signifying her dad's phone was at the horse farm down the road. "He hid your keys so you wouldn't try to leave, but he didn't hide *my* keys."

Dani sat up and rubbed the sleep from her eyes. She looked at the clock on her nightstand. "It's one a.m."

"I know."

"No, why is Dad at the horse farm this late at night?" She knew he liked the farm, but she had no idea he liked to go there in the middle of the night.

"That's a long story for another time. Right now, get dressed in something cute and get your butt out of here."

Dani reached for the lamp on her nightstand, but her mom told her to keep the lights off.

"Even though he's down the road, he might see a light on. He won't think to check if my car is here since we keep it in the garage. Hurry up, honey."

Dani had a hundred questions, but mostly she was excited to get to see Neo. She dressed quickly in jeans and a top and put on her favorite tennis shoes. "My phone," she said. "Plus, I just realized I don't know where he lives, only where he works."

"Here it is," her mom said, handing her the phone. "Text him you're on the way to the park. I know he'll meet you there."

Dani looked at her curiously as she took the phone and turned it on. "How do you know?"

"Listen, there are few things in this life that we can be certain about. The sun will always rise. The tide will ebb and flow. And when you meet the man who's supposed to be yours forever, nothing should stand in the way of that." Her mom let out a sharp breath and then said, "What you described about meeting Neo is exactly how I felt when I met Dexter. Now Dexter's got some opinions about what your future should look like, and no amount of me telling him it's not fair to pull you away from Neo right when you met him will change his mind. So I waited until he was gone, and here we are. Go to Neo. Tell him that your dad and brother, and probably the other four knuckleheads, will be at the park in the morning. He'll know what to do."

"Mom, I'm totally confused."

"It'll make sense soon enough, honey. I can't tell you what you need to know, you have to figure it out for yourself. Just like I did."

"Now I'm really confused."

"Then go find your man."

Dani brushed her teeth, grabbed her wallet and phone, and followed her mom down the stairs. Dani didn't take the long dirt road that went by the horse farm, instead driving the long way around to the main street. She sent a text to Neo that she was on the way to the park and needed to see him. Then she put her foot on the gas and hoped her dad didn't realize she was gone until she was safely with Neo.

CHAPTER SEVEN

Neo was pacing in the family room of his house, his beast clawing at him to go find Dani. It was well after midnight, and his nerves were frayed. He hadn't heard from her since she left, and while it was only a handful of hours since they'd said goodbye it felt like an eternity. After the eye-opening and disturbing conversation with the alphas, he'd tried to work on park vehicles, but he'd been unable to concentrate on anything but Dani.

He wished he hadn't had to let her go.

August cleared his throat, and Neo looked over at him. His friend and fellow gorilla shifter was giving him a long look from where he sat on the couch.

"You're going to wear a hole in the floor."

"I know," Neo said. "I can't sit still. I've got a tenuous hold on my beast at best, and the only thing that seems to keep him from forcing my shift and finding Dani is keeping moving."

"I'm sorry you're so torn up," August said. "It sucks."

"It's late. You should get some sleep."

"Atticus said one of us needed to be with you at all times to make sure you don't do something idiotic, so I'm staying."

While it rankled his beast to be watched over like a wayward child, he also appreciated his friend watching out for him. "I don't want to do anything idiotic, trust me. I'm just frustrated."

"Of course you are." August gave him a curious look. "You really think she's a shifter?"

"I don't know." Neo blew out a breath and put his hands on his hips. "Part of me doesn't. She reacted as if she didn't see me as anything but a man. But maybe? There's definitely something off about her family."

His phone buzzed, and he pulled it from his pocket, surprised to see a text from Dani.

I'm on my way to the park. Can you meet me there?

Of course. Go down the side road that says employees only. I'll meet you at the guard station.

I'm about an hour away. I'm sorry I had to leave. My dad was acting crazy.

It'll be okay. Just drive safe. I'll be waiting.

"I gotta talk to Atticus," Neo said after telling August about the texts.

"Let's go wake up the alpha," August said, pushing up from the couch and smiling broadly. "Your soulmate is on the way, man. Congrats."

"Thanks."

Ten minutes later, Neo was standing at the guard station of the employee access road that ran alongside the park. Atticus was waiting with him.

Footsteps alerted Neo to someone approaching, and he was surprised to see Joss and Caesar. He knew that Atticus had alerted the alphas that Dani was on the way to the park, but he hadn't expected any of them to come topside.

After greeting them, Joss said, "We've got wolves

patrolling the exterior of the park as well as the apartment complex. While we can hope that she's got her family's blessing to come here, I think it's safe to assume that she doesn't, and we need to be prepared for anything."

Neo didn't want to think that her family might be against them being together–had even hoped they might have had a change of heart–but he knew it was better to err on the side of caution. Particularly since it seemed likely that she'd needed to sneak away.

His hopes were high. She was coming to him. Whatever happened with her family, they'd deal with together.

He faced the three alphas. "What does it mean for where she can stay tonight? The rules are pretty clear."

Atticus's brows rose, and he looked at Joss and Caesar for a long moment. "We need to tread carefully because we have no idea what the situation is with her family. We've got some cots we could bring up into the employee cafeteria," Atticus said.

"Can't I just tell her what I am?"

"The only way you can do that is if she confirms that she's a shifter or knows about shifters. There's too much at stake for you to simply tell her and hope she doesn't freak out and want to leave," Caesar said.

"All right," Neo said. He didn't like it, but he understood.

Atticus called for a few of the gorillas to bring cots up from storage and set them up in the cafeteria. It wasn't going to be ideal, but at least she'd have a place to sleep and Neo could watch over her.

It seemed like forever, but he finally felt her drawing close and saw headlights turning down the service road. His heart in his throat, he watched her car approach and then slow until it stopped. She turned off the car and got out.

"Neo!"

~

Dani had never felt so relieved in her life than when Neo met her on the road and hugged her. He squeezed her tightly and lifted her off the ground. She buried her face in his neck and tried not to cry. She'd been fighting tears since she left home. She didn't like running from her dad or hiding things from him, but she was equally certain he was hiding things from her, too.

"You okay, sweetheart?" Neo asked with a rough voice as he set her feet on the ground but didn't relax his hold.

"No. Yes. I guess?" She blinked to dispel the tears and brushed at her wet cheeks. "I'm glad to be here with you, but I'm freaked out about my dad's behavior."

"You remember Joss?" he asked.

She looked behind him to where Jeanie's husband stood with two other men. "Sure."

"That's Atticus and Caesar," he said. "They work at the park, too. They're here because we're concerned about things with your family and want to make sure you're okay."

She blew out a breath and leaned away, breaking contact with him to look at the three men. "Hi."

They each greeted her.

Joss cleared his throat. "Can you tell us what's going on with your family, Dani?"

"Could we do this somewhere more comfortable, like the cafeteria?" Neo said.

"Sure," Atticus said.

The men led the way into the park and to the employee cafeteria. The lights were low in the large room. It was full of tables and chairs, but a section had been cleared and two cots were in the open space. Neo led her to a table and pulled out a chair for her.

"Can I get you something to eat or drink?" he asked as she sat down.

"Yeah," she said. "I didn't feel like eating earlier."

"I'll see what's up here."

Neo hurried away to a kitchen area while the three men sat across from her at the long table.

"Your father and brother were quite angry earlier," Joss said. "Was it because of the tour or something else?"

"The tour," she said. "I don't understand why, but he and my brother were really insistent I didn't go on it or even into the park at all. When I asked them for an explanation, they said they'd tell me everything Monday night."

"What's happening Monday night?" Caesar asked.

"My parents are hosting a party for some of my dad's friends from out of town."

"Is your family from this area?" Joss asked.

"My mom and I are, but Dexter and Khyle aren't."

"He's... not your biological father?" Neo asked as he set a tray on the table in front of her. There were two sandwiches—one ham and one turkey—a bowl of pasta salad, a bowl of fruit, and a plate with a cookie and a brownie on it. He'd brought a soda and a bottle of water as well.

Her stomach growled, and she realized how famished she was.

"No. My dad died when I was a baby. Dexter married my mom when I was two. Khyle was his son from a previous relationship. But I think of them as my real family because they're all I've ever known."

"Did they ever lead you to believe that there was anything unique about them?" Atticus asked.

She unwrapped the ham sandwich and took a bite, mulling over what he said. "Do you mean like a secret identity or something?"

The man nodded.

She shrugged. "Not really. But I've had a weird feeling lately that they're not telling me everything about themselves. Like a situation in the family has changed and I have to figure it out for myself."

"How did you get here tonight?" Neo asked. "Did you have to sneak out?"

"My mom woke me up and gave me the keys to her car and my phone–my dad had taken it from me. She told me that how I felt about you is how she felt about Dexter, and that my dad was just being stubborn and not listening to me. She said I had to figure this situation out for myself. I'm feeling pretty confused and frustrated, frankly."

"That's understandable," Neo said. He put his hand on her shoulder and gave it a comforting squeeze.

She took a few more bites of her sandwich and washed them down with the water. "By the way, my mom said to tell you guys that my dad and brother, and maybe the four guys in the crew, will be here for sure in the morning looking for me. She didn't want you to be caught off guard."

"I've reached out to Dexter several times," Joss said. "He won't return my calls."

"I know he's not home right now, or at least he wasn't when I left."

"Do you know where he is?" Atticus asked.

"At the horse farm down the road from our house."

Everyone looked at her in confusion.

"He likes horses. He has a deal worked out with the farm owner to help out with them. My mom said that he goes there at night when he can't sleep."

"Well, whenever he shows up," Joss said, "we'll be here. In the meantime, it's very late. We arranged for some cots to be brought up here so you and Neo could rest."

"It's okay for us to be here in the park like this?" she asked.

Neo tossed her water bottle in the recycle can and threw her trash away. When he returned to the table, he said, "You're looking at three of the owners of the park right now, sweetheart. So yes, it's perfectly okay for us to be here."

"My mom said you wouldn't have a problem meeting me here," she said. "So it seems like she knew you lived either in the area or.... do you live here?"

"Yes, I do," Neo said.

"Yes, you do what?"

"I live here in the park."

"But the apartment complex isn't finished yet."

"We have other living arrangements," he said.

"Why can't we stay there?"

Neo opened his mouth but hesitated.

"There are regulations in place for who can stay in our employee housing," Atticus said. "So for now, this is the right place for you two to be. The windows are one-way glass so no one can see in, and we'll leave a note on the door to let employees know they shouldn't come in here until after you two are awake. Otherwise our food service staff will be waking you up at dawn to stock the cafeteria."

"Okay," she said. "Thank you."

The three men left, and Neo locked the door behind them.

"Can I get you anything else?" he asked.

"No, I'm good, thanks." She stood from the table but didn't know what to do.

Neo joined her and took her hand, bringing it to his lips with a smile. "You doing okay, sweetheart?"

She really liked that he called her sweetheart.

"Yeah. Frustrated, though."

"That's understandable." He took her to the cots, which had thin mattresses and were stacked with pillows and blankets. He sat on the cot against the wall and patted the space next to him. She sat, feeling the weight of the situation with her family settling on her shoulders.

"You know what sucks, though?" she asked.

"What?"

"That they came after me like they did. I've never been so mortified in my life. They made me feel like a child, like I couldn't trust myself to make my own decisions."

He was quiet for a moment, then said, "I don't think you should feel that way. Your family was just looking out for you. While we don't know what their reasons are yet, they obviously love you and want the best for you. There isn't anything wrong with a family looking out for their own. My mom would storm the gates of hell for me, whether I wanted her to or not. And even though I'd like to think I'd be a cool dad, I'm pretty sure I'm going to be the most overprotective male on the planet."

Something deep inside her ached when he mentioned kids, but she pushed the wishful thought away. "I'm not saying that I don't appreciate my dad, I just wish he wasn't so heavy-handed. Or that he'd tell me what's really going on."

She stifled a yawn, her eyes burning with exhaustion.

"Let's try to rest," he said. He leaned in and kissed her, but it was over far too soon.

He got up and moved to the other cot, which was just a foot away from where she sat. After setting up the blankets and pillows, they both stretched out. She kicked off her shoes and turned on her side, facing him.

He was so sexy. She'd never been more attracted to a man in her entire life. It made her angry that her dad was trying to keep her from him without giving her a full and honest explanation. She didn't think there was anything he could tell her that would make her understand.

She wasn't sure she'd be able to fall asleep, but then Neo moved the cots next to each other and put his hand on the curve of her waist. He smiled at her, and it was the sort of unspoken promise that said he'd never let anyone take her from him again. She didn't know how she knew that, but she felt it all the way to the center of her being.

As her eyes slowly closed, she thought she saw his eyes change color from blue to brown.

There was something very familiar about the color change, but she was too tired to put the pieces of the puzzle together.

CHAPTER EIGHT

Neo snapped to awareness sometime later with his soulmate snuggled up against him on the cot. He didn't know when she moved over, but it was still dark outside, so he didn't think they'd been asleep too long. She was lying half on him and half on the edge of the cot, her head resting over his heart and her hands twisted up in his shirt. He wasn't sure what prompted her to join him, but he was glad she did.

She made a soft sound and rubbed her cheek on his chest. His body sprang to life, and he bit back the groan as she wiggled a little against him.

He wished he could tell her what he was. Show her. But things were so up in the air with her family that he didn't dare put her in a position where she'd have to go against her family to stay with him. He was sure her family was hiding a shifter secret from her, but since he wasn't one hundred percent positive, he couldn't take the chance to show her what he was.

Damn he hated there was an untruth between them.

Her hand slid purposely down his side and reached the

waistband of his jeans. Her fingers pushed under the edge and his bare skin screamed for more touching. He grasped her wrist as her hands moved toward his navel.

She giggled softly and tilted her face toward him.

"Hey," she said softly, her eyes alight with a mixture of humor and seduction.

"I thought you were asleep."

"I was." She twisted her hand in his grip and linked their fingers, bringing their hands to her lips and kissing his knuckles. "I had a weird dream and woke up. Hope you don't mind I joined you."

"Not even a little bit. Was it a bad dream?"

"I don't remember it, actually, I just woke up and realized I'd been dreaming. I think it's stress."

"I'm sorry, sweetheart."

She let go of his hand and planted hers on either side of his head. "I'm only sorry things are so crazy. There's so many things I wish were different right now."

Her legs parted on either side of his hips as she stretched out over him, her upper body a few inches from his, her gaze searching.

"Like what?" he asked.

"Like I wish I didn't live at home, so you could have come to my place. Or that there weren't rules in the park, and I could've stayed with you instead of on the cots. Or that I'd met you years ago."

He cupped her face and brought her to his lips for a kiss. "I wish for all of those things, too."

She tilted her head and tried to deepen the kiss, but he eased away from it and rolled them to their sides.

"Why did you stop?" she whispered.

"Because we're on a cot in a cafeteria, and while I'm certain no one is going to disturb us for a while, I don't want to go any further and risk someone seeing you."

She frowned. "Why?"

"Because I'm already feeling protective of you and we've only kissed, sweetheart. If someone tried to come in here and we were doing more than just talking and holding each other, I can't say that I wouldn't go on a rampage."

She chuckled and snuggled closer to him. "I understand."

"Good. It's not that I don't want to be with you, because there's nothing I want more."

"It's not ideal," she said. She let out a sigh and rested her cheek on his biceps.

His beast was clamoring in his mind to get back to the kiss and whatever else the beauty had in mind, but he knew he wasn't wrong. It was wildly unfair to move forward physically when there was so much she didn't know about him.

A grunt of annoyance rumbled in his chest as he pushed his beast away, and she sat up with a gasp.

"What's wrong?" he asked, rising up onto his elbow.

"That sound you just made."

He wondered if it sounded really animalistic to her. He hadn't meant for it to happen.

"Just clearing my throat." Damn, that lie was bitter on his tongue.

"No, it's not just the sound, and I know you're lying to me. Your eyes just changed color right now, and I saw it before I fell asleep earlier." She climbed off the cot and stood next to it, her hands on her hips and her eyes blazing with indignation. "Tell me I'm not going crazy."

He rose to his feet, a few inches between them. Was it possible? Did she really know what he was?

"What do you think's going on here, Dani?"

"I think I'm going bananas."

He nearly laughed at the phrase. Bananas? Yes please.

He didn't know how to proceed. His hands were proverbially tied on what he could say to her. She had to figure it out for herself.

"You're not crazy, Dani." He moved until they were nearly touching, and he could feel the heat of her body and pick up her naturally sweet scent. "Tell me what you're thinking, and I promise I won't take you to the loony bin."

She blinked rapidly a few times and then looked down, her shoulders dropping. "When I was on the tour, I really liked Neo the gorilla. It was so weird, because he's a gorilla, you know?" She lifted her head and looked into his eyes. "I couldn't explain it, but I felt like I was supposed to be on that tour, and that he was the reason. His eyes changed color, too. From brown to blue and I felt like he was trying to communicate with me. And then I met you in the office and your name is Neo, and your eyes changed color. But from blue to the same chocolate brown of the gorilla."

She stopped speaking for a long moment and just stared at him. Fuck she was so close to the truth that he almost blew his cover and told her everything right there. Instead, he said, "Say it, Dani."

"It's too crazy."

He cupped her face. "Say. It."

Her hands wrapped around his wrists. She inhaled then blew the breath out sharply. "You're the gorilla."

Dani half expected Neo to laugh his ass off or tell her she was the nuttiest person he'd ever met. But when she'd spoken what was on her heart, she just knew that it was the truth. As fantastical as it seemed, as crazy as it sounded, Neo could become a gorilla.

Right?

He hadn't actually confirmed or denied what she said.

She opened her mouth to ask him if she was right, when he grinned and kissed her.

"You're right," he said, his eyes turning brown.

"I'm right? Are you serious? How is that possible?"

He sat on the cot, and she sat on the other, facing him. "Shifters are real, but our natures are a secret from humans. That's why you don't know about our kind."

"There are more of you out there?"

With a nod, he linked their fingers. "Yes. There are different types of shifters and they all live in secrecy."

Her mind spun. Then something occurred to her. "You live here."

He nodded. "Underneath the park."

"Wow." She ran a hand through her hair with a laugh, the weight off her shoulders. "It's a relief to know. I honestly thought I was cracking up."

"You're not. You feel drawn to me, right? The way you did to the gorilla?"

"Yes."

"It's because I *am* that gorilla. My people believe in soul-mates–the one right person for us. Someone our beast agrees is who we should be with."

"You said you asked Jeanie about me."

"Right. My gorilla was agitated, and I followed the feeling to the office where I picked up your scent. I knew you were my soulmate. Joss wouldn't let Jeanie give me your contact information, so I had to wait until you came by on the tour. It was the longest time of my life."

"Why wouldn't he?"

He told her how the park had set up the VIP tours to bring in unmated males and females, hoping for soulmates to be among those who received the coupons in the mail. "He wanted me to do this right, and for that to happen, it was best for me to be in my shift."

"All those gorillas in the paddock with you, they're human, too?"

He nodded. "The alpha is the leader and the others are my friends. We handle the maintenance in the park. I work on the park vehicles including the Jeeps for the tours."

She hummed. "What is Joss?"

"A wolf. Caesar is a lion."

"Geez, I really can't believe it. It's so fantastical, but it also feels very right." She rubbed the space over her heart. "I feel like I've known this for ages, but it's not possible. Do you think my dad and brother know about you guys and that's why he didn't want me to go on the tour?"

"I don't know. It certainly seems suspicious that he actively tried to keep you away from here. He never gave anyone any hints that he knew we were more than human, though, so if he did..." His voice trailed off.

Dani finished the thought. "You think he's a shifter?"

"I don't know, sweetheart. And that's the honest truth."

She mulled that for a bit and then shook her head. "When he shows up today, I guess I'll ask him. Maybe this is what he's been hiding from me lately. Which means my mom knows about it, which is why she wanted to help me out by letting me come here. Man, I hate that I feel like I've been lied to."

"I'm sorry."

She waved her hand dismissively. "I understand why you kept the shifting secret from me. It's too dangerous for you to just tell anyone without knowing what their motives are. That you're unique and that's why I feel so drawn to you is amazing, and I feel really lucky."

"Trust me, sweetheart, I'm feeling really, really lucky, too."

She sighed wistfully as she looked around the room.

He tugged on her hand. "What's that for?"

"I wish we weren't here. I wish we were in a more private place."

She also wished neither of them were wearing clothes, but she kept that part to herself. For now.

He took his phone from his pocket and said, "Let me see if I can do anything about that." He swiped the phone's screen and then gave her a very serious look. "If we do this, sweetheart, if we go somewhere private and things happen between us, you won't be able to leave the park. At least not until the alphas are satisfied that you're willing to keep our secret."

She inhaled deeply, her thoughts roaming. "I'd need to quit my job. But I wouldn't be able to tell my parents why I won't be home anymore, and my dad would know that there aren't any apartments available in the park for me to live here. Unless he's also a shifter, or knows the truth, then that puts me in a position to lie to my parents."

"I don't want you to have to lie, sweetheart, but if we go forward physically, I won't be able to stop myself from mating you fully and that means my gorilla isn't going to want you sleeping anywhere but in my arms. If your parents try to get in the way of that, I have to know that you're going to pick me."

"I will."

"Even if it means you might harm your relationship with them?"

She nodded. "You're my guy, Neo. I don't want to be anywhere but with you, and I want to be yours in every way." She pursed her lips for a moment and then said, "Can you come with me to my parents' house, though? I mean, if my dad still wants me to meet with his friends, would you come so I could do that?"

"Of course."

"Then yes, let's go somewhere private."

His eyes flashed to that brown she loved, and he lifted his phone to his ear. "Hey Atticus, did I wake you? Oh, good. Listen, Dani knows the truth now, and she'd like to be somewhere more private. Could I bring her down to my house for the rest of the night?"

Neo winked at her, and she smiled.

"Okay, thanks." He put his phone on his knee and said, "He's going to check with Joss and the other alphas, but I don't think they'll say no."

They waited a few minutes, and then his phone buzzed with a text. He looked at the screen. "Atticus said as long as you understand that you can't be away from me overnight–even if it means going against your family–then you can come down to my place."

"Tell him I understand completely."

"I can't tell you how happy I am," he said, smiling as he answered the text. It chimed again and he said, "Atticus is going to come to talk to us first, and then we'll be cleared to go down."

He rose to his feet and pulled her with him. "I'm really happy, too," she said. "But I think we're about to be a whole lot happier."

"Abso-fucking-lutely."

CHAPTER NINE

Atticus met Neo and Dani in the cafeteria ten minutes later. Neo was a bundle of nerves, his gorilla pacing in his mind and anxious to get her into their home.

"I hope we didn't wake you," Dani said.

"You didn't, actually, I was up reading. So before we go any further, I need you to tell me what you know, Dani."

"I know that Neo is a gorilla."

Atticus smiled. "How did you reach that conclusion?"

She blew out a breath. "It was a combination of things. Mainly, though, it was because when I saw him in his gorilla form in the paddock, his eyes changed color and I felt weirdly drawn to him. Then when he met me in the office and he said his name was Neo, which is what I was told the gorilla's name was, I first thought it was a prank. But then Neo's eyes changed color, and even though I didn't believe what I was seeing, I felt it in my heart."

Atticus's brows rose. "The tour guide told you what the gorilla's name was?"

"Uh huh. Was he not supposed to?"

"I just didn't realize that he did."

"Did he tell you any other names?" Neo asked.

"He told me a couple of the wolves' names. And then he apologized to you and said your name."

Neo nodded and looked at Atticus. "I haven't been on a tour with the wolves, but it sounds like they don't mind telling the riders our names."

"I think they shouldn't do that," Atticus said. "But I don't know if Joss knows they do that either. I'll speak to him later this morning. In the meantime, Dani, did Neo explain what's happened now that you know our secret?"

"That I can't be away from him overnight."

"Right, it'll drive his gorilla nuts. You're not officially mated yet, but I can already see how connected the two of you are."

Neo took Dani's hand and gave it a squeeze. When she looked at him, he said, "I think that Atticus is making sure you understand that no matter what your family says, you and I are together now and that means where you go, I go."

"Except overnight of course," Atticus said.

"Right," Neo said. "I can't stay away from the park overnight."

"I get it," she said. "I don't want to be away from you. But if my dad asks me to come to the house, and I can bring you with me, is that okay?"

"You'll need an escort," Atticus said, rubbing his chin. "But yes."

"I'd like to get my sweetheart down to the house so we can rest," Neo said.

"Of course. The patrols know to expect your family. We'll let you know when they show up. We'll be bringing them in here for privacy sake."

"Thanks," Neo said.

"I'm glad you two found each other." He smiled and headed toward the door that led down into their underground living space.

Neo gave Dani's hand a squeeze and followed his alpha. When they were in the gorillas' private living area, Atticus said goodnight to them and left the two of them alone. Dani turned in a slow circle, taking in the room.

"Holy crap," she whispered. "This is incredible."

He smiled. "I'm glad you like it."

He led her to his home, atop the steel and bark-covered fake tree. "How do we get up there?" she asked.

"There's a set of stairs I can let down, but I think it would be more fun to carry you up there this first time."

Her eyes narrowed. "Carry me how?"

He dropped to one knee and pointed to his back. "Climb on."

She did, wrapping her arms and legs around him. He rose to a crouch, his gaze on a branch above their heads. "Hold on, sweetheart."

He leaped for the branch and caught it, swinging them up into the faux canopy. She stifled a small scream of surprise and then giggled. He moved onto the platform that supported his home and walked inside.

Shutting the door, he helped her off his back and said, "Welcome home, Dani."

She looked around the front room the same way she had in the main living quarters, turning in a slow circle, her eyes wide. The family room had a dark brown leather couch and a wooden side table with a lamp. He'd hung a flat screen TV on the wall and added some bookshelves for his knickknacks. He liked to collect antique car parts.

She walked to the bookshelf and peered at his collection. "Are these parts for anything in particular?"

"Not really, just older models that I liked the way the pieces looked."

"I like to collect carousel horses. It started with one I got from my dad on my fourth birthday. Every year after that he's gotten me one, and we look for them on vacation, too."

He smiled. She turned to face him, and her voice dropped to a husky tone. "Can I see your room?"

His whole body reacted, his gorilla hooting in his mind. "I need to share something with you first, sweetheart." He sat on the couch and patted the cushion next to him. She joined him and gave him a curious smile.

He cleared his throat and took her hand, linking their fingers. "You know what I am. Because I'm not entirely human, my reactions to you won't be what you're used to."

"Like what?" she asked, her brows arching.

"Well, when I'm really happy my gorilla will hoot, and sometimes I can't stifle that sound. I wouldn't want you to be scared or startled by any sounds I might make."

"Do you pound your chest when you're angry?"

"When I'm in my gorilla form, yes. Not when I'm human, though."

She grinned and gave him a quick peck on the lips. "Okay. I promise not to be freaked out by any sounds you make."

"Also, though we're heading toward the bedroom, maybe we won't do anything tonight or maybe we will. But if we do, Dani, my beast is going to want to mark you. That means using my teeth to bite your neck to leave a scar. I'll have to let my beast out a little to make my teeth sharp. It will hurt some, but I will do my best to distract you with pleasure."

He put his free hand on her neck and lightly pressed his thumb to her pulse.

"Why?"

"It's a mating bite," he said. "It's a way for my beast to

claim you in a primal way. Any shifter who would see the mark would know that you're mated."

"Mated like we had sex?"

"No, mated like married. It's why I couldn't just take you back to the bedroom without telling you what it means to be with me. My gorilla wants you so much, that I'd have a hard time not biting you while we make love. I'd never do anything without your permission, so I'd rather not make love to you tonight if you're not ready to be mine. And when I say 'be mine,' I mean you'll essentially be my wife."

She looked at him intensely for a long, quiet moment. Her gaze dropped to their joined hands and then slid up to his neck. "Do I get to bite you?"

His beast liked that idea a hell of a lot. "You can do anything you want to me, sweetheart. But your teeth aren't sharp, so it would just leave a bruise. Which I would love and wear with pride."

She chewed on her bottom lip, her gaze meeting his. "Do you want to do that to me? Do you want us to be married?"

"Since the moment I scented you in the office," he said. "But you're not used to this. For me, it's the instinct of my beast to make you mine as soon as possible. But I'm in control, not him, and I'd never try to pressure you. We can wait until you're ready."

"What if I'm ready now?"

"We just met, sweetheart," he said gently. "We don't have to rush."

She straddled him suddenly, sitting on his thighs and cupping his face. "I felt drawn to you when you were in the paddock even though it felt weird. I can't explain it, but knowing that you're that gorilla makes me feel like I was destined to find you. Soulmates is a romantic notion for humans, you know? But I feel like it's very real for me and you. I want to be yours in every way. When we meet my family, I want to be able to tell them that you're mine."

"I am, Dani," he said. "I'm yours all the way to the center of my being."

"I'm yours, too. Neo?"

She leaned forward, her eyes darkening.

"Yes, sweetheart?"

"Make me yours."

CHAPTER TEN

Neo gave Dani the most intense look she'd ever seen. She felt like she could burn alive under his gaze and love every second. It had been the craziest day of her life, from the strange behavior of her family to the tour to finding out that there were people who could shift into animals whenever they wanted. She still had a million questions about his people and the safari park, but the only thing she was certain of at that moment was that she wanted to make love to Neo and be his mate.

He gripped her hips and pulled her against him. She could feel the ridge of his erection, and her body went tight and hot. She leaned in for a kiss and he took over, wrapping his arms around her and holding her tightly as he deepened the kiss. Shivers raced over her skin as their tongues danced together, her stomach flipping with anticipation. She moved her hips and he groaned, bringing a hand up to tangle in her hair. He tilted her head and deepened the kiss.

She slipped her hands down his sides and fisted the material of his shirt. She'd been dying to see what he looked like without his shirt on, and now that they were finally somewhere private, she wanted to see all of him. Pulling from the kiss, she tugged on the shirt and pulled it from his waistband. He straightened and grasped the back, pulling it swiftly over his head and tossing it aside. He settled back on the couch with an arched brow, looking all cocky and sure.

She grinned and laid her hands on his abs, feeling the taut, smooth skin. "You're so sexy. I can't even tell you how much I wanted to scc you naked."

"The feeling is wholly mutual."

She traced the ridges of his abs, feeling like she'd never get tired of touching him.

She pulled her shirt over her head and dropped it with his. He made a happy grunting sound, and she met his gaze with a smile.

"Now who's the sexy one, sweetheart?" he asked, his voice low and gruff.

He cupped her breasts, his thumbs tracing the lace edge of her bra. Her skin goosebumped under his touch as he moved lazily over her cleavage, his gaze dark and intense. She reached to the decorative bow between the cups and unhooked the clasp. He spread the cups open, moving slowly up the straps and pushing them off her shoulders. She wiggled free of the material and then let out a moan as his warm hands closed over her breasts. He moved one hand to her back and drew her close, lowering his head and catching one of her nipples between his lips. He licked a slow circle around the bud sending shivers down her spine.

She wrapped her arms loosely around his shoulders and played with his hair, closing her eyes as the sensation of his lips on her nipples made everything within her heat. He teased her nipples, tugging and nipping at them until her body was aching for more.

He rose to his feet suddenly, cupping her bottom and holding her close.

"Bedroom?" he murmured against her skin, his face buried in her neck.

"Hell, yes."

He chuckled in a manly way, like he knew just how wild he was driving her and he liked it.

She did, too.

He carried her down the hall and turned into the first bedroom on the right. The room was dark, but he seemed to have no trouble navigating his way to the bed. He bent down and laid her on a soft blanket, and then there was a click and a low light on a nightstand illuminated the room with a soft, golden glow. He put his hands on the waistband of her jeans with a heated smile and undid them. Then he tugged the material down her legs, catching her panties in the process. He stopped at her ankles and removed her shoes and socks, then stripped her entirely bare.

She rose onto her elbows and smoothed her hair away from her face.

He straightened and placed his hands on the waistband of his jeans, giving her an arched brow.

"You, too," she said, surprised at how husky her tone was.

"As you wish, sweetheart."

He undid his jeans and shoved them down his legs, toeing off his shoes and stripping fully. He planted his hands on the edge of the bed on either side of her legs and looked up the length of her body.

"You're it for me, Dani," he said. "I just want you to know that I've waited my whole life for you, and I'll never let you go. You're mine and I'm yours."

His words were intense but not frightening. She felt the same way.

"You're mine, too."

He nodded with a soft snarl, his eyes flashing to brown. He grasped her ankles and spread them slowly, pushing gently until she bent her knees. She'd never been so laid out bare before a man before, but she liked it. Liked how intensely he was looking at her, as if she were the only woman in the whole world and his happiness rested with her.

She had to spread her legs wide to make room for his broad shoulders. He kissed his way up her legs, alternating from one to the other, until he was heading down her thighs toward her pussy. She stretched out on her back and laid a hand on top of his head as he reached the apex of her thighs, his warm breath skirting over her folds. He settled between her legs and curled one hand under her hip and spread his fingers across her abdomen. As he spread her open with his fingers, she could hear him inhale and then nuzzle her wetness. He stroked up her folds with his tongue and let out a groan.

"Fuck, Dani," he said, his voice harsh and deep.

Her toes curled at his tone, the demand and pleasure rolled together in the way he said her name. She didn't think any man had ever wanted her as much as Neo did.

He tilted his head and lapped at her entrance, then slowly licked up to her clit, circling the bud before delving back down. He made the pass again, faster, his tongue sweeping past her in swift movements, a flick here, a lick there, too much and not enough at the same time. Her hand curled into his hair, her nails scraping his scalp as he feasted on her. She wanted to beg him to let her come. She wanted to demand he never stop.

Instead she just moaned his name.

He snarled softly, and then he laid his tongue against her clit and growled. Her whole body lit up at the sound and the vibrations that tingled through her. He pushed first one finger and then two into her as he played with her bud, a riot of sensations cascading through her as he drove her to the peak of pleasure. The center of her body went white hot and she came, her eyes rolling back in her head and her back bowing as she cried out his name.

He kissed up the center of her body and curled his hands under her shoulders, pulling her down onto his hard length and meeting her with a swift thrust. He was thick and long, and he waited a moment before he slowly pulled out and then thrust in again. As her body adjusted to him, she met his thrusts, lifting her hips and pulling him faster into her by hooking her ankles together.

He kissed her, and she groaned into his mouth, everything feeling too good and too much. Too everything.

She never wanted it to end.

He began to move faster, their kiss breaking as the power of his thrusts left her breathless and wanting more.

He pushed his hand under her hips and lifted up, changing the angle of his thrusts until his cock rubbed something within her that made her gasp in pleasure.

His eyes were hooded, his fangs peeking from his lips as he clenched his teeth and drove into her. Faster and deeper.

Rubbing that spot again and again.

Pleasure swirled in her core, and she let go, coming so hard that her vision blurred and she felt like her bones had melted from the intensity.

He roared when he came, his cock pulsing within her.

She was dimly aware of his snarl a moment before his fangs sank into her neck. She gasped at the sensation that was a combination of pain and pleasure. The connection she'd felt to him when he first entered her solidified in her mind, and she wrapped her arms around him as he removed his fangs from her flesh and kissed underneath the aching mark.

"I know it's early, Neo," she whispered, her voice raw from screaming her pleasure, "but I'm so in love with you."

He lifted enough to look at her, his eyes the brown of his gorilla. "I love you, too, Dani."

He snuggled up next to her and tugged up the sheet to cover them. With his arms around her, the fresh mating bite in her neck, and the truth of what they now were to each other, she felt safe and secure, and loved. And she'd never been happier.

Dani heard something buzzing as she woke, her mind a pleasant haze of sleepiness and contentment. As she slowly pulled herself out of the sleepy stupor, she realized that the buzzing sound was a phone.

"Neo?" She sat up and shook his shoulder.

His eyes opened, and he said, "Hey, sweetheart."

"Hey yourself. I think your phone's buzzing."

He sat up when the buzzing happened again. "Yep. The question is, where is my phone?"

With a laugh she said, "I don't have any idea."

He climbed off the bed and rummaged through their clothes on the floor, finding his phone in his pants pocket. He swiped his thumb on the screen and lifted it to his ear. "Hey, Atticus. What's up?"

He joined Dani on the bed and put the phone on speaker.

"Sorry to wake you two, but Dani's dad, brother, and the four guys from the construction crew are here. Dexter is demanding to see her immediately."

"They're in the cafeteria?" Neo asked.

"Yes. But don't come up through the interior entrance, come topside through the maintenance shed and walk to the cafeteria. We don't want them to realize there's an underground space where we live."

"Okay. We'll be up as fast as we can."

The call ended, and Neo twisted on the bed to face her. "Sorry we didn't get much sleep. I was hoping they wouldn't show up too early."

She looked at the screen, seeing it was six thirty.

"Do we have time to shower?" she asked.

"No, it'll take too long. We've got a bit of a walk, so let's just get dressed and get up there. I've got a spare toothbrush for you."

After she got dressed in her clothes from the day before, she used the bathroom and brushed her teeth. Her hair was a ratty mess and her makeup had rubbed off, so she ran a brush through her hair and washed her face.

She found him on his phone in the kitchen. "I only have regular coffee," he said, pointing to two travel mugs. "Nothing fancy or flavored. We can order whatever kind of stuff you like from the market for delivery or we can go shopping."

"I'm okay with regular coffee."

She used milk and sugar to fix it the way she liked and then put on the lid.

They left the house. Neo lowered the stairs so they could walk down.

"You really just swing yourself up there all the time?" she asked.

"Pretty much. Unless I have stuff I need to carry. We can keep the ladder down, so it'll be easier for you to get into the house."

"I didn't mind the ride," she said, smiling at the memory. Although scary at first, she'd enjoyed it when she got over her initial surprise. "But the ladder would be helpful if you weren't with me and I needed to get into the house."

"Exactly."

They walked to the far wall of the private living quarters, and he entered a code into a security door, which opened to a hallway and a flight of stairs. At the top of the stairs, he lifted the ceiling up which turned out to be a door in the floor of the maintenance shed.

When they were inside the shed, he closed the door. "This is where I spend most of my days. Except for the weekends when I'm in my shift for the tours."

"Will you still have to be out there during the tours even though you're mated?"

She could feel the healing mating mark and she smiled.

"Not all the time, but sometimes, yes. Two of the guys have soulmates who are human, and they sometimes put on zookeeper uniforms and walk around the paddock during the tours so it looks more realistic. Adriana has a nail salon in the marketplace under the park, and Lexy runs the candy shop topside. Atticus will probably set up a dinner so you can meet everyone."

"Oh, I'd like that."

He led her to the door of the shed. "Which part?"

"Both. I'd like to see you be your beast again, since I didn't get to spend a lot of time with you."

"We can totally do that." He put one hand on the door. "Before we leave, remember that the secret of the park has to stay with you. You can't tell your family anything about us."

"If they ask where I stayed last night?"

"Tell them in the cafeteria, and that we were up early and in the maintenance shed when they showed up. You can go home to pack your things, but I'll be coming with you, and we can't stay away from the park at night."

"I wish the apartment complex was done."

"Me, too. Your family will just have to trust that you're making the right choice for yourself. It would be nice if you could tell them what we are and why you have to stay here, but..."

She nodded. "I totally understand, and it's okay. I don't

want to put you or anyone in the park in jeopardy. I've never given them a reason not to trust me, and judging by what my mom said about understanding how I felt toward you, I think she'll be supportive of us. My dad, on the other hand, appears to be acting like a lunatic right now."

"I've got your back, sweetheart."

"Let's go see what my dad has to say," she said.

Neo opened the door and took her hand, and they walked out of the shed together. The early morning sun illuminated the park, and she inhaled and rolled her neck, hating how much she felt like she was going to war with her family. She'd never expected her family to be against her like this. The only solace she had was that her mother seemed happy to help her.

The door of the cafeteria opened with such force that the glass cracked down the middle. Her father stood in the doorway, his face a mixture of fury and disappointment.

Neo took a step in front of her, acting as a shield.

Caesar rounded the building and said, "That was highly unnecessary, Dexter."

"I want to know why you're here, Danielle Marie, when I expressly forbid it," Dexter said, ignoring Caesar and stalking toward her.

The way he called her by her full name made her stomach turn.

"Dad," she said.

He stopped a few feet from them. Khyle and his four friends joined them.

"Answer me."

She felt Neo tense, could see the way his muscles bunched up like he was barely holding onto his control. Atticus, Joss, and a few other men she didn't know appeared, some coming from inside the cafeteria and some from the direction of the security office. She quickly stepped between her dad and Neo.

"This is so over the top, Dad," she said, rubbing her temple. "What the heck is wrong with you? I'm not a child, I'm an adult. And before you say, 'you live under my roof,' I'll just remind you that I'm being respectful to you. You're the one acting like a whackadoodle. Stomping over here, demanding to see me like I was abducted from my bed or something. For crap sake, Dad. What did you think the end result of you coming at me like this would be? That I'd walk away from a man I'm in love with just because you said so?"

She planted her hands on her hips and glared at her dad, and then glared at the five behind him, one after the other.

Neo put his hand on her shoulder, and she glanced at him.

She slowly faced her father again. "You need to tell me what's going on. And be honest."

Her father's angry glare was replaced with a frustrated look. Khyle stepped up next to him.

"We should perhaps go somewhere more private," Khyle said.

"Back into the cafeteria?" Dani suggested.

"Actually," Khyle said, "I think we should go into one of the animal paddocks."

Dani frowned. "What? Why would we do that?"

"You want us to trust you, so you need to trust us," Khyle said.

"The bears' paddock is empty," Joss said. "It's the closest one."

"Lead the way," Dexter said.

As they walked to the path leading to the tour, she thought over what she'd learned after spending time with Neo. During one of their chats in between making love, he'd told Dani about the different shifters who called the park home. Lions, elephants, wolves, bears, and gorillas. Each one had their own private living space under the park, and they all worked together to make it safe for themselves. She was overwhelmed with the knowledge that there were so many different kinds of shifters and humans were none the wiser.

She looked over her shoulder at her family. It wasn't just Dexter and Khyle, but Crew, Grey, Ford, and Avi who she considered brothers as well. She'd grown up with them all, and Dexter had always appeared to be like a father to them, too.

Slowly looking back to the path, she frowned as she thought about her childhood. She didn't know anyone else who had friends who were so close like the guys were to Khyle and her dad. There was something that connected them together, and for a moment, she thought about Atticus and Neo.

Atticus wasn't Neo's father. He was his alpha, the gorilla leader. While Atticus's son Zane was an only child, Neo said that Atticus was like a father to all of them. He was a rule enforcer, a friend, a father figure.

Just like Dexter.

She couldn't help but wonder...

CHAPTER ELEVEN

N eo could tell that Dani was deep in thought as they made their way to the paddock. He wasn't entirely sure what was going on with her family, but he suspected they were about to get a revelation in what they truly were. He hadn't told Dani his suspicions about her family, but he wished he had. He'd been counseled by the alphas to keep his thoughts on the matter to himself because if they were shifters, he'd out them, which wasn't right. Or if they weren't, he could ruin Dani's faith in them. Just like she'd come to the conclusion that he was a shifter, she had to reach that herself about her family.

Atticus unlocked the gate into the paddock and pushed the door open. Everyone entered, and the gate was shut behind them.

"We've got some privacy now," Dani said. She faced her father, and Neo stood next to her.

Dexter looked at his son and the four males with them and shook his head. "I can't do this."

"I'll do it," Khyle said.

"You know what our laws are," Dexter said. "I know why

you wanted privacy, but this still crosses a line I can't cross. You know that."

"What the heck is going on?" Dani asked. "Someone please tell me."

Neo put his arm around her and drew her close. The alphas and several other shifters were standing with him and Dani. He was thankful for their support. Especially when the other males were acting so oddly.

Khyle pulled his shirt over his head.

"What are you doing?" Dani asked.

"Showing you the truth."

She looked at Neo in confusion. He shrugged.

As Khyle undid his jeans, Neo knew that he was going to shift into something. What it would be, he didn't know, but judging by the looks on his dad and friends' faces, he wasn't supposed to be doing it in front of strangers.

"You know what I'll have to do, Son," Dexter said. "Think this through."

Khyle gestured to Dani. "She's hurt and angry, and all because of an archaic law. She's with a damn shifter. She'll keep our secret, too."

Neo's brows rose. "It's true then. You know what we are."

"Yes," Khyle said.

He shucked his jeans and took a large step back. In moments he went from a man to a horse.

A huge, black-coated horse with a black mane and long, sweeping tail.

"Holy shit!" Dani said, her voice a high squeak of surprise.

Khyle rose onto his hind legs and let out a sharp whinny, his hooves slamming into the dirt with a loud clap.

Neo was dumbstruck. A horse shifter? He'd never heard of such a creature.

He smelled salt water and realized that Dani was crying. "You okay, sweetheart?"

She shook her head. "Dad? I don't understand. You're a horse shifter?"

Dexter hung his head and sighed deeply. "I wasn't allowed to tell you, because our laws forbid us from sharing the truth of our shift with anyone but our soulmate. It's grounds for immediate exile. And we don't call ourselves horses, we're stallions." He lifted his head and rubbed the back of his neck. "Damn it, Khyle."

The big stallion snorted and pawed at the ground.

Crew shook his head and slapped him on the hindquarters. "Jackass. What the hell are we supposed to do now?"

"There's only one thing I can do," Dexter said. "Either I exile Khyle or I disband the herd."

"What the fuck?" Grey demanded. "No one has to know, Dex. You don't have to do this."

Dexter tapped his temple. "My beast won't let me. You don't understand what it means to be lead stallion. The laws are ingrained in me. You four can go on your own way and start a new herd."

"But we're family," Avi said.

Dexter put up his hands. "I will not discuss herd business at this time. For now, Dani, Khyle has shown you the truth. We're stallion shifters. Only males are born, so we find our soulmates in humans or other supernatural creatures. Each herd has its own alpha. We never, ever share our nature with anyone but our soulmate. But, in cases where a human is a soulmate, and a female child is born, she would be told the truth because she's half stallion."

Dani wiped at the tears on her cheeks. "Mom knows?"

"Of course."

"You couldn't tell me because your horse won't let you?"

"Yes."

"Then why could Khyle?"

"Because he's always hated the secrecy. You're the only

family he's ever known, and it killed him to lie to you so much."

She left Neo's embrace and walked to her brother. She tentatively rested her hand on his neck and stared up at him. Then she gasped. "I know you. I rode you! The horse farm is... for you?"

Dexter nodded. "The farm belongs to us. We use it as a cover to shift. Whenever you wanted to go to the farm, a few of us would shift so you'd be able to see horses there and not be suspicious."

She pressed her head to Khyle's neck. "I'm utterly destroyed. My whole life feels like it was built on a lie."

"I'm sorry, honey, truly. We were hoping that one of the males from the herd visiting tonight would be your soul-mate, so you'd be able to learn the truth."

She sniffled. "That's why you were so insistent on me meeting with them."

Ford said, "Don't hate us, Dani. We didn't like lying to you either."

She looked at Neo. "Did you know they were shifters?"

He shook his head. "We thought something was up with them because of the way Joss said they acted about your VIP tour." He looked at Dexter. "You don't smell like a shifter though."

"It's just a perk of being a stallion. To other shifters we smell human."

"When did you know about us?" Joss asked.

"Well, we didn't until we got to the park. Devlin's human. But the park smells like all kinds of predator shifters," Dexter said.

"You could have come to us as fellow shifters," Atticus said.

"Surely you have rules your people have to follow," Dexter said. "We're no different. I could no more tell you than I could tell Dani. It's been hell for her mother and me to keep the secret from her. So much lying, so much covering our tracks to not arouse suspicion."

Dani patted her brother's neck and then returned to Neo's side. "Why were you so against me coming on the tour?"

Dexter didn't say anything for a moment, and then he said, "Because I wanted your soulmate to be a stallion. You're human, so I didn't know if you'd be swayed by meeting other shifters, even if you didn't know what they really were. When I got home last night, your mother was waiting for me and told me what she'd done."

"Are you done being pissed?" she asked.

"You found your soulmate in a male who's willing to go against six males to protect you. So yes, I'm done being pissed. I was never really angry with you, Dani. You didn't know what was going on. I'm just... it was always my dream for you to find a stallion soulmate so you could be with your family."

"I can still be with you," she said. "We're still family even if I'm mated to Neo."

"But the herd isn't going to be the same," he pointed out. "Khyle has forced my hand, and I have some decisions to make."

Joss stepped up. "I never knew stallions were real. It's quite amazing. How long does Khyle need to be in his shift?"

"A few hours."

"Why don't we get some breakfast in the cafeteria and talk while we wait?" Atticus said.

"I need to call your mom," Dexter said. "But yes, that would be fine with us. Crew?"

"I'll stick around with Khyle. Anyone got some carrots?"

"There should be some fresh produce in the maintenance shed," Caesar said, "I'll take you over."

Everyone headed toward the fence to exit the paddock, but when Dani didn't move, Neo looked at her. She was staring at her brother, whose ebony head was down, his gaze on her.

"He's still him in there," Neo said, brushing a lock of her hair behind her ear.

"I know, it's just surreal. My brain's trying to reconcile everything in my childhood with what I know now."

"Are you angry with them?"

"Yes and no."

He chuckled. "It's okay to be angry, but don't hold their secrets against them. Shifters have a different code than humans. There are things we can't, or won't, do to ensure the safety of our people. Your dad has clearly wrestled with keeping you out of the loop."

"If Khyle hadn't shifted…" Her voice trailed off.

"You might never have found out," Neo said softly.

She looked up at him with a sad smile. "Yeah." She sniffled and rubbed her eyes with the heels of her hands. "Shit, I'm exhausted."

"Totally understandable," Neo said. "You've just had your whole world turned upside down. Twice."

She let out a short laugh. "Right. First shifters are real, and then I find out my family are shifters, too. Thank goodness my mom's human. I'm not sure I could handle another crazy revelation."

Crew came back to them with a bunch of carrots tucked under one arm and a few apples in his hands. He offered an apple to Dani. "They're his favorite. Wanna feed him?"

She stared at the red fruit in silence.

Caesar cleared his throat. "Secrecy is part and par of what we are. But no matter that Khyle is a shifter, he's your brother first."

She lifted her hand slowly to Khyle. He took the apple from her hand and swiftly devoured it. She rubbed his nose and said to Crew, "Which one of you has white patches on his legs?"

"Ford," Crew said.

She looked at Neo and said, "Once when I was twelve, I was walking around the farm's paddock and picking dandelions for Mom. A few of the horses were milling around. Then the one with white patches came barreling toward me. He grabbed the back of my shirt and lifted me into the air, then stamped his hooves into the ground. He was whinnying so loudly that my ears were ringing. Dad came running from the barn, and the other horses raced over. Dad took me from the horse and looked where he'd been stomping his feet." She looked at her brother and Crew. "There was a rattlesnake a few feet from where I'd been picking flowers. Ford saved my life."

"He did," Crew said, "but he couldn't tell you it was him. You were scared to go into the paddock after that happened, even though we'd all swept the area and made sure there were no other snakes around. Then Ford took your hand and walked the paddock with you, said you didn't need to be afraid, because you had five brothers who would do everything to keep you safe."

She hugged Khyle's neck and then hugged Crew. "I'm glad I know the truth now. And I need to thank Ford for saving my life all those years ago."

"So you don't hate us?" Crew asked with a smile as he offered Khyle a carrot.

"Nah. I love you guys. We're family."

"One hundred percent."

"What do you think will happen with Dad and you guys because Khyle shifted?" she asked.

"I honestly don't know. But I do know that Khyle doesn't

regret shifting so you'd know the truth. Hell, I was a few seconds away from doing it myself."

"I'm glad he did."

"I think we need to catch up to Dexter and the others," Neo said, taking Dani's hand. "Call or text Dani when he can shift back, and we'll come let you guys out of the paddock."

"Will do," Crew said.

Caesar left with Neo and Dani, and they headed toward the employee cafeteria.

"Is there a shifter court or something?" Dani asked as they followed the path.

"What do you mean?" Neo asked.

"Dad said there were laws in place to prevent Khyle from shifting, and that he'd have no choice but to disband the herd. So is there a group of rulers who enforce the laws for each shifter group?"

Caesar, who'd been quiet as they walked, said, "No. The alpha of the group is the law. Now in our situation, the alphas form a counsel and arbitrate issues for the common good, but it's still up to the individuals to police their own kind."

"If there's no one who will come down on them for it, why can't he just move on as if Khyle didn't break one of their rules?"

"Because he's alpha," Neo said. "Atticus says that being alpha means that he has to make calls that others might find distasteful or cruel, but his beast won't let him slide on some things. And a rule like not shifting in front of non-shifters is definitely on the list."

"This is complicated," Dani said. "I don't know if it's better that I know what's going on or if I was actually happier before I knew that Dad and the guys are also harboring this secret."

"I think it's better to know," Neo said. "Now they don't have to actively keep things from you."

"That's a good point," she said.

They reached the employee cafeteria. Neo held the door for her and Caesar, and then followed them inside. Several of the tables had been pushed together to create one long one, and trays of breakfast foods had been set across the center.

The stallions were seated on one side of the tables. Dani sat across from her dad, and Neo sat next to her.

"I'm sorry, Dad," she said.

"Why are you sorry?"

"Because you might have to break up the herd because of me."

"No," he said, reaching across the table and taking her hand. "I should've told you years ago, laws be damned. But I was afraid that I'd lose the herd if I told you, and the boys are like my sons. I just kept hoping you'd find a stallion soulmate so we could all be together."

"Can't we still be together?" she asked.

"Of course," he said. "You and your mom are family to me and Khyle, and nothing is ever going to change that."

She gave her dad's hand a squeeze. "Do you need me to come to the party tonight? So the other herd doesn't know what happened?"

Dexter's brows rose. "I already spoke to the other alpha and canceled the meeting. I told him you were in a serious relationship and I couldn't in good conscious bring them in with the express purpose of meeting you. It wouldn't be fair to Neo to subject you to a party designed to hopefully pair you off with a stallion."

"Good." Dani gave Neo a smile. "I really didn't want to go, but I would have to keep the peace."

"I appreciate that, but it's not necessary," Dexter said.

Dani's stomach took that moment to growl loudly and

her cheeks pinked as everyone laughed. "Sorry! I haven't had anything to eat yet this morning."

"Well, let's not let this food go to waste," Dexter said. "It looks great."

They all agreed, and while Neo was certain that Dani had a lot more questions for her dad and the other males with him, she nodded in agreement. As Neo held the heavy platters for Dani so she could fill both her plate and his, he explained that the bear shifters handled all the food, from the employee cafeteria to the food stalls within the park.

When they'd eaten their fill, the alphas left Neo, Dani, and her family and friends alone in the cafeteria to wait for Khyle to join them. Dani's mother, Nancy, showed up, and Neo was glad he had an opportunity to meet her and thank her for helping Dani to come see him.

"Well, I know a soulmate connection when I see one," she said. "Even if others are too stubborn to."

Dexter made a face. "I said I was sorry, love."

"I know, but I'm still going to lord it over you for a while."

"Great," Dexter said, shaking his head with a smile.

An hour later, Khyle and Crew joined them. Dani hugged her brother. "Thanks for spilling the beans."

"You're welcome. You have no idea how often I wanted to shift and show you the truth." He looked at Dexter. "I'm sorry, Dad. I didn't want the herd to disband, but Dani had a right to know."

"I know," Dexter said.

"Are you going to kick Khyle out of the herd?" Dani asked.

"I'll still be part of the family," Khyle said. "It's not like he'd disown me."

"I know, it just sucks." She blew out a breath and crossed her arms. "I think you're a great leader, Dad. And Khyle's a great brother."

"I need some time to think on everything that's happened," Dexter said. "In the meantime, I think we should head home."

"What are your plans?" Nancy asked.

"I don't know," Dani said.

"Well, I haven't asked her yet, but I'd like for Dani to move in here with me and live in the gorillas' private living quarters. I'm not allowed to give you a tour, just know that she'll be safe with me," Neo said.

"I know she will," Dexter said.

"I'd like to live here." Dani smiled at Neo.

"You can come pack a bag," Nancy said. "And we can pack up your room for you."

"Can we do that tonight, Neo?" she asked.

"Absolutely."

They walked Dani's family and the herd members out to the parking lot and said goodbye. Dani and Neo stayed until they were gone, and then she turned to him. "This has been the craziest couple of days."

"It has, hasn't it?"

"Can we go home?"

Neo frowned. Where did she mean when she said the word home?

"I mean," she said, "can we go down to your home? I'm tired as hell."

"It's *our* home now, sweetheart."

"Then let's go to our home."

"You got it."

CHAPTER TWELVE

Later that night, Dani moved around her bedroom, packing two suitcases with clothing. Her parents had offered to pack bags for her ahead of her visit, but she'd politely declined, knowing they were busy dealing with Khyle's revelation and what it meant to the herd.

The herd! The thought that her family had been shifters all along and kept it from her still made her head swim.

"Do I need to take hangers, too?" she asked Neo as she pulled a shirt from a velvet hanger.

"Yeah, I don't have many."

She set the hanger on top of the others on the bed. Neo stood at the window and looked out. "That's the farm?" he asked.

"It is. Khyle and the guys are there now. We can stop by on our way out."

"Your dad seems really upset." Neo turned and faced her, crossing his arms.

"I think so, too. I don't understand what the big deal is. It's not like I'm going to tell anyone, and for sure the shifters in the park wouldn't either."

He shrugged. "Stallions are clearly unique. Something about being alpha is making your dad want to disband the herd because of what Khyle did." He got quiet for a moment and then said, "I can't imagine having a child and not telling them the truth of what I am. It's living a lie. He must have constantly worried about slipping up and telling you something he shouldn't."

"Well, to be fair I'm not his biological child."

"He treats you as if you were."

"Good point." She mused on what he said. "I wonder if his desire for me to know about what he and the others are is why he was so insistent I not go back to the park until after the get-together with the other herd?"

"I'm sure it is. From what he and your mom said, he's been banking on you being a stallion's soulmate since he married your mom. Even the best taught child can be a ticking time bomb with sensitive information. He must've been afraid of Khyle telling you something or you figuring it out."

She folded the shirt and placed it on top of the others. As she walked to the closet, she said, "I get it and I don't get it. Once I became an adult, I think he could have told me the truth. It makes my heart hurt that he didn't think he could trust me."

"You don't understand being a shifter, sweetheart. You're my soulmate, and I wanted to tell you the truth the moment I met you. I couldn't, because I didn't know how you'd react. If you tried to leave, the alphas wouldn't have allowed it, and then there would be a bigger problem. Imagine how Dexter felt, always having to keep you out of the loop. And your mom, too."

"I'm not saying it wasn't difficult," she said, gathering several dresses. She paused and turned to face him. "I need to quit my job?"

He raised a brow. "Are you asking me or telling me?"

"I don't know."

He chuckled and then sobered. "I don't want to tell you what you can and can't do, but if you want to continue to work at the cosmetics store, then I'm going to insist on driving you there and back. My beast would rail against anything else."

"I started working there when I was sixteen," she said. "What would I even be able to do at the park? It's not like I know how to fix cars and could work with you in the maintenance shed."

"I'd teach you, but I don't think you really want to learn." He joined her, taking the clothes from her and draping them over the suitcase. He put his hands on her hips and brought her close to him.

She really loved when he held her like that.

"Not really," she said. She put her hands on his shoulders, feeling the strength in his muscles. It was tempting to shut the bedroom door and push him to the bed, but her parents were in the house, and she'd come to learn that her dad had excellent hearing because of his shifter genes.

Neo squeezed her hips, and she met his gaze. "I can tell you're thinking sexy thoughts, but don't forget your parents are in the house."

She tried to feign innocence. "How would you know what I was thinking?"

"First," he said, leaning in and kissing her lips gently. "You smell turned on, like your sweet scent is on overload, extra sexy and amazing. Makes my gorilla want to do things to you."

She shivered. "What things?"

"Wonderful, dirty, sexy things."

"How else can you tell what I'm thinking?"

"Your eyes darken. But aside from that, I'm also thinking sexy thoughts, and it seems like we're in-sync in that respect."

She rose onto her toes and kissed him more fully, then eased away. "We should hurry and get home, then."

"You have the best ideas," he said with a grin.

"So back to my job," she said.

He nodded. "I'd like to ask you to quit, but I won't. If you want to keep working there, I'll drive you. It's not a problem."

"I just don't know what I'd do if I wasn't doing makeup," she said.

His gaze narrowed, and she could tell he was mulling something over. She loved how his brows lowered and he pursed his lips when he was deep in thought. He was so sexy. She wasn't sure how she'd been so lucky, but she was thankful he was in her life now.

"I have some ideas, love, but I don't want to say anything until I have a few conversations with some people."

"That doesn't sound suspicious at all," she said, rolling her eyes.

"I know, I know," he said. "I'm sorry. I don't want to get your hopes up if I can't work something out for you, but I'm going to do my damnedest to make you happy."

"I already am happy, Neo. You're the best thing that ever happened to me."

"You, too, sweetheart."

They finished packing, filling up the two suitcases with clothes, a duffel with her makeup supplies, and a trash bag with velvet-covered hangers.

"Ready?" he asked at the doorway.

"Yes."

She took one last look at her bedroom and then walked into the hall, closing the door. She stared at the polished wood and a sign that Khyle had made for her with her name on it. The bubble letters had been hand-carved and painted in her favorite pastel colors. She took it off the hook and tucked it into the bag with the hangers.

Downstairs, she hugged her parents. Dexter looked both happy and sad, but most of all he appeared stressed. His blue eyes were tight at the corners, and while he was smiling, it looked forced.

"Dad, are you okay?" she asked.

"I will be, honey, don't worry."

"I feel like I totally messed up your lives. I don't regret finding Neo, but I hate that Khyle had to shift and broke your rules."

"You don't need to worry," Dexter said. "I promise that we're still your family and nothing is ever going to change that. The moment I knew your mom was my soulmate, you became the daughter of my heart. You found your soulmate, and I couldn't be happier for you to be with such a caring, protective male. I don't hold you accountable for anything that happened, you were following your heart. That's all I ever wanted for you."

She hugged him tightly, her eyes stinging with tears. "You're the dad of my heart, too."

"Khyle asked if you'd stop by the farm on your way out to say goodbye," her mom said as she accepted another hug.

"Okay," she said.

Her parents walked them out, Dexter opening her door as Neo put her things in the back of the SUV. Dexter spoke to him quietly and then joined her mom on the porch. Neo climbed behind the wheel and backed out of the driveway. They waved at her parents and she said, "What did he say to you?"

"That even though we're soulmates, if I ever hurt you, he'd bury me somewhere I'd never be found."

She barked out a laugh and shook her head. "Oh my gosh."

"Hey, he's your dad. It's his job to threaten. I plan to do that if we have any girls."

She smiled at him. "The boys better watch out if we do."

"You know it." He winked and pressed on the gas, accelerating down the road and then turning into the farm.

She couldn't believe she was going to the farm to talk to her brother and the guys she'd thought of as her adoptive brothers, knowing that they were horse shifters. While part of her harbored some annoyance at not knowing the truth until now, she wasn't going to hold it against them. If she'd been tasked with a secret to keep from her family because it would keep her soulmate safe? She'd totally keep them in the dark. She was just glad she hadn't needed to.

Whatever happened to the herd because of Khyle's law-breaking behavior, she knew she wasn't responsible for it. The laws–however archaic she felt they were–were in place for a reason, and she couldn't take the blame for what happened. She was just grateful Khyle had broken the law so she knew the truth. She'd never be the same, but it seemed that the herd wouldn't be the same either.

She met Neo at the front of the SUV and took his hand.

"I'm so glad you're mine, Dani," he said. "I'm thankful you went on the tour even though your family was strongly opposed to it."

"Me, too."

"Love you," he said, his voice low and growly.

"I love you, too." She kissed him and smiled. "Let's say goodbye to Khyle and the guys fast and get home."

He gave her a sexy smile. "There you go, having great ideas again."

She wiggled her brows. "I'm full of great ideas. Fair warning, most of them involve being naked."

"Did I say great ideas? I mean the most exceptional, best ideas on the planet."

With a wink, she gave his hand a squeeze, and they headed toward the big red barn to say goodbye.

CHAPTER THIRTEEN

Neo and Dani had spent a week holed up in their home in the gorillas' private living quarters. When they'd emerged at the end of the week, the love he'd felt for her when they'd mated the week before had strengthened and deepened. He was one hundred percent head over heels for his soulmate, and excited to see what the future held for them. She fit right in with the gorilla band and Adrianna, Zane's human soulmate, and Lexy, Win's human soulmate.

He'd left his sweetheart with the two females in the marketplace that morning to enjoy breakfast, and had gone to speak to Anke and Zeger, the wolf couple who operated the marketplace's supply store.

"Morning," Zeger said when Neo walked up to the counter.

"Hey," he said, shaking his hand. "Thanks for meeting with me."

"Anytime," he said. He motioned with his hand, and Neo followed him into the little store.

When Dani had asked about continuing her job at the cosmetics store, part of him had wanted to demand she immediately quit and glue herself to his side. The possessive and protective male in him didn't want her away from the park, and even though he'd promised to drive her to and from work, he knew he'd be a wreck waiting for her. He would do it, though, to make her happy.

But he'd had some ideas on how to make her happy within the park. He'd texted with Atticus during their week-long sequestering, and his alpha had been instrumental in speaking to the other alphas and approving the ideas he had for his sweetheart. When she'd told the store that she was taking a week's vacation, they'd not been happy about it. They were expecting her to return on Monday. If she liked any of his ideas, then she'd be able to give her notice to the store and have a job waiting for her here.

He wanted her to be safe, but he wanted her to be happy, too. He'd never put his foot down and demand she do one thing or another that went against what was in her heart. Her happiness was paramount to him. Period.

"Good morning, Neo," Anke said. She turned from a shelf where she was dusting wireless speakers with a cloth. "How was your honeymoon?"

"Awesome and over too soon," he said as he took a seat at a little table in the back of the store.

"That's so sweet," she said as she joined him and Zeger at the table. "I'm excited about your ideas."

Neo breathed out a sigh of relief. "That's great news."

"We got the okay from Joss to do whatever we need to make this happen but give us the full rundown so we can make sure we're all on the same page."

Neo nodded and took out a large piece of paper from his back pocket, unfolding it and spreading it out on the table. He'd asked Mercer, one of the lions, to draw up plans for an addition to the nail salon in the marketplace which was next to Anke and Zeger's store.

"Here's your store," he said, pointing to it on the blue-prints. "The lions will cut a hole through this wall and open the space between your store and the nail salon. They'll build up the area between your store and the nail salon to create a place for Dani to sell makeup and do makeovers." He pointed to the new area, which he envisioned would be lined with lighted glass shelves and have at least one chair and mirror set up for her to do makeovers. Dani would have the final say in what the store looked like of course, but he'd worked out the bare bones of what they needed to get working.

"We don't mind losing part of that wall," Zeger said, looking up past him to the wall that would become an archway into the cosmetics store. "When Joss told us about the remodel, we thought it was a good time to go through the stock and get rid of anything that hasn't moved off the shelves in a year or more."

"I'm happy to help with anything you need," Neo said.

"I'm happy that things are changing in the park," Anke said. "First, they added the nail salon down here, which we all love. And now to have makeup and a person who can make us all look lovely–well, I'm in heaven."

"I like the candy shop," Zeger said.

"Me, too," Neo said. Win's mate, Lexy, was a baker by trade and ran the topside candy store, along with her best friend Trina, who was mated to Justus, one of the bears.

"I hope more of our people find their soulmates," Zeger said. "It's been too long for so many."

"I heard that more people have signed up for tours since they sent out the VIP tickets a second time," Anke said. "That's a good sign in my book."

"Definitely," Neo said. While his situation with Dani wasn't quite the same as what the alphas expected to happen with the VIP tour tickets, she had come on the tour and he had known she was his soulmate. It just happened that she'd been given a ticket by Jeanie and hadn't received one in the mail.

However she'd come to be his, he was grateful.

Rising to his feet, he shook both their hands. "Thanks for being so willing to help with this."

"We're happy to," Anke said.

"Just name your firstborn after me and I'm good," Zeger said.

Neo chuckled. "I'll have to run it by the boss."

"You know it," Anke said with a wink. "Always check with the mate before making life-altering decisions. It leads to a longer, and happier, life."

"Happy mate, happy life," Zeger said. "That's true of any species."

Neo left and returned to the marketplace, where Dani had finished breakfast and was adding sugar to her coffee. He kissed her cheek and sat next to her, greeting Lexy and Adriana.

Lexy looked at her watch. "I need to scoot, or Trina is going to lord it over me that she's at work before me."

"Save me some dark chocolate sea salt caramels," Dani said.

"You bet."

"That's my cue, too," Adriana said, taking a last drink of orange juice. "I've got a nine o'clock French manicure."

"Don't forget to put me in the book," Dani said.

"I won't. I'll send you a reminder text." Adriana waved and left, heading into the nail salon.

"Did you have a nice breakfast?" he asked.

"Yep. How was your meeting?"

"Good. We've got some time before we need to leave to see your parents. I wanted to take you on a real tour of the park if you'd like."

"Oh, really? I'd love that."

She exchanged her regular coffee mug for a travel mug and poured her coffee into it. They headed topside to the employee cafeteria and took a leisurely walk around the park. They spent the most time at the bird sanctuary, run by Jess and Auden. They lived in the converted barn next to the sanctuary that doubled as a bird hospital. After visiting with Jess and Auden, they finished up the tour at the candy shop, where she took a wrapped package of caramels from Lexy.

"Who are those for?" Neo asked Dani as they headed toward the parking lot where the employee vehicles were kept.

"Dad. They're his favorites."

"That's sweet," he said.

"Well, he's been kind of cagey about what's going on with the family, and I know I'm going to hear about it today. I can tell he's stressed and so is Khyle."

"Heavy is the head, darlin'," he said.

"I guess so."

They talked a little on the drive to her parents' house, but she seemed mostly lost in thought, and he let her have the silence. He pulled into the driveway, noticing that there were a few more vehicles parked there than he'd expected.

"I think all the guys are here," she said.

Neo opened her door and took her hand. The front door opened, and Khyle greeted them, his eyes tight and his lips in a thin line.

She hugged him. "Everything okay?"

"Yes and no. We're waiting for you, though. Dad wouldn't tell us anything until you arrived."

Dani gave Neo a worried look. He wanted to reassure her that everything would be fine, but he had no idea what her father was going to say.

They followed Khyle into the family room. Dani hugged her parents and each of the males, and Neo greeted everyone.

"Here, Dad," she said, handing him the box.

He opened it and smiled at her. "Thanks, honey. You're so thoughtful."

Placing the box of candy on the coffee table, Dexter settled back on the loveseat and put his arm around his mate. Neo and Dani sat on one of the couches, squeezing on the end next to Khyle.

"All right," Dexter said. He didn't speak for a moment and then cleared his throat. "Damn it, this is hard."

"Dad," Khyle said.

"Nope, no," Dexter put his hand up. "I get to speak now."

Khyle let out a grunt and clicked his teeth together.

Dexter stared at the guys one by one, and then looked at Dani. "I'm so happy you have your soulmate and know the truth of our people. I know you're learning about the laws that govern us and ensure our secret remains hidden from humans, but I also know that you don't really understand what it means to be a shifter and particularly what it means to be alpha."

Dani nodded but remained quiet.

"Sometimes, tough decisions–ones that seem unfair on the surface–must be made. And I've had to make one of those decisions. I don't come to this conclusion easily, but it's for the best for our people." He paused, looking like he was trying to compose himself. Then he continued, "I'm going to step down as alpha."

All five of the stallions voiced loud objections. Dexter put his hand up, and they went quiet, but Neo could feel the anger emanating from them.

"It's the only way to preserve the herd," Dexter said. "I've pored over the laws since it happened, and I have only two choices. I either step down as alpha or I exile Khyle. This way, you can choose a new alpha and the five of you can go on as a herd, and Khyle won't have to be without his people."

"Dad," Dani said. "Why can't you just overlook what he did or punish him or something? I don't understand why you have to do something so drastic."

"Because you're not a shifter," Dexter said.

"Well, I think that's bullshit," she said.

"Language!" her mother said.

Dani rolled her eyes. "Mom, seriously! You can't tell me you think it's the right choice! The herd should stay together, with Dad as alpha. Did you even ask the guys what they wanted to do? Look at them! They're upset, especially Khyle."

"Because I'm the one who caused this mess," Khyle said.

"Because of me," Dani pointed out.

"Stop it, both of you," Dexter said. "No more trying to accept blame or make this situation easier. The reality is that when I chose to become alpha and start my own herd, I accepted the responsibility of upholding the laws. One of the main ones we have is that we don't shift in front of humans unless they're our soulmate. While what Khyle did was noble and the true definition of family in my book, it doesn't change the law that he broke."

Khyle rose to his feet. "I don't accept this, Dad."

"You don't have a choice, or a say, in what I do as alpha," Dexter said. "I make the decisions, and I'm stepping down. You can still use the farm to shift, we'll still have the construction company, and we'll still be a family. But I won't be part of the herd, period."

"No." Khyle stared at his dad and then looked down at Dani and Neo. "If I leave the herd, do you think I might be able to find work at the park?"

Neo stared at him in surprise. Before he could answer, Dexter stood. "What do you think you're doing?"

"You're not at fault here, Dad–it's me. I made the choice to shift. I exposed us to the other shifters, and to Dani. And we discussed it last night," Khyle said, gesturing to the other males. "Even if you step down, whoever takes over as alpha will still know that I'm a liability. No matter how much they want to keep our herd going, I'm going to need to walk away to preserve it. This way, you're still alpha, and I can still work with you at the construction company and finish the park apartment project, but I'll just be your son, not under your authority as leader."

"It's true," Crew said. "If you step down as alpha, one of us would have to step into leadership. It couldn't be Khyle, because our stallions won't follow someone who flaunts the rules like that. I don't know who among us would be alpha, but if it were me, I'd want Khyle gone anyway. As harsh as that sounds. If he's not part of our herd, though, we can still stay together, and he can work with us. He just needs to find another place to call home."

"I can't be alpha anymore," Dexter said, shaking his head. "Khyle leaving doesn't change that."

"Maybe not," Grey said, "but we can still stay together. You exile Khyle, and as your last act as alpha, you recuse yourself. The four of us will be a herd, we'll move into the farm, and you can use it to shift with us and we'll still work for you. Nothing else has to change."

"But Khyle won't be in the herd anymore," Dani said.

Neo cleared his throat. "But he's my family now, too. There's a paddock of normal animals. We could easily bring a stallion into the mix. As far as living arrangements, that's something the alphas would have to decide, but I'm sure we can find a place for him. When the apartment complex is finished, he could stay there maybe, and then he could work somewhere in the park."

Khyle looked relieved. "Thanks, man."

Neo nodded. "Dexter, I'm not alpha and I have no idea what you're dealing with. But it seems like what your stallions are suggesting is what would work best for everyone."

Dexter let out a deep sigh and pinched the bridge of his nose. He lifted his head and looked at each of his stallions. "Are you certain about this course of action?"

"We're sure," Avi said.

"Then let's go to the farm." He stood and looked at Neo and Dani. "Thank you for your help and support, but this is as far as you can go."

"Stallion business," Dani said. "We get it."

She rose to her feet and hugged her dad, then hugged each of the stallions, ending with Khyle. "We'll talk to the alphas and let you know what they say."

"Thanks, Sis."

Khyle nodded at Neo, then followed his father and the others out of the house.

"Well," her mother said. "That didn't go at all how I thought it would. But it sounds like it's all going to work out. Do you really think the alphas will let him live and work there?"

"I don't see why not."

They stayed at the house for nearly two hours, waiting until Dexter returned. When he arrived, Khyle and the others weren't with him. They'd stayed at the farm to shift one last time.

"You're not alpha anymore?" Dani asked.

"Nope," he said. "It's strange but also a relief. It's stressful being a leader. I'm thankful to just be the construction company boss now."

"And my soulmate, don't forget," her mother said with a smile.

"That's the best job on the planet," he said. He kissed her mom and then looked at Dani and Neo. "Thanks for coming to support us. It means the world to me now that I can share this part of my life with you, Dani."

"Me, too."

They said goodbye a short time later, and on the drive back to the park, Neo got a text from Khyle asking if he could make arrangements to talk to the alphas, and he promised he would. Once they reached the park, Neo parked in the employee lot and took Dani's hand as they walked through the security gate and headed toward the employee cafeteria.

"It's been a crazy night," she said. "I can't believe how much my life has changed in a short amount of time."

"You're okay with everything?" he asked. "It can be overwhelming to learn so many things you thought you knew actually aren't what they seem."

He opened the door to the cafeteria, and she stepped inside. "I'm good. In a way I feel like I knew all along that Dexter and Khyle, and the others, were keeping something from me. It was just a thought in the back of my head, but it was there. It must have been hard for them to lie to me."

"I'm sure it was."

"I'm glad that we don't have to keep secrets from each other," she said.

"Me, too."

Once they were back in the gorillas' private area, Neo spoke to Atticus about the situation with Khyle and the stallions, who agreed to discuss it with the alphas. The alphas had never brought in a person in Khyle's situation into the park to live. Everyone who was living underground was either a soulmate or part of one of the groups. The question Neo thought would be brought up was whether a stallion could pledge his allegiance to an alpha who wasn't his shifter species, and if he could, who he'd declare fealty to.

He walked into their home, where he'd left Dani so he could speak to Atticus privately, and was surprised that she wasn't in the family room. They'd talked about watching a movie and relaxing.

"Sweetheart?"

"In here," she called.

He followed the sound of her voice to the bedroom, his gorilla hooting happily to find her stretched out on the bed wearing her bra and panties, a sultry gleam in her eyes.

"You look like you have wicked things on your mind," he said, his voice gruff.

"Always," she said. "Tomorrow you have to go back to work. I wanted to celebrate the last night of our vacation."

"That's the best idea I've heard all day," he promised, toeing off his shoes and stalking toward his soulmate. She was everything he'd ever wanted and many things he hadn't known he'd needed. She fit with him perfectly, and he adored every inch of her. His life had changed forever the moment he'd scented her, and he'd never forget how lucky he was to have her in his life.

CHAPTER FOURTEEN

For the last month, Dani had been working around their little house during the day while Neo was in the maintenance shed. Dani had quit her job at Beauty after their honeymoon. While Neo said he was okay with driving her back and forth for work, she didn't feel right being away from the park and didn't like the strain she could see it was causing him.

She had loads of free time, so she'd painted the master bedroom, learned how to install new fixtures in the bathroom, and taken some sewing lessons from one of the wolf females on how to make curtains, which she'd hung in the family room. While she loved keeping busy with those projects, she'd also done some makeovers for shifters, taking her makeup with her. She missed working at the cosmetics store, but she was happy to be able to help the few ladies who asked for her expertise to look their best.

"Hey, sweetheart," Neo said, stopping in the spare bedroom she'd set up for her makeup supplies.

"Hi," she said, smiling brightly. She swiveled on the padded stool and rose to her feet.

He pulled her close and gave her a hug. "You busy?"

"Never when it comes to you. What's up?"

"I wanted to go to the market."

"Oh."

He gave her a curious look. "Are you disappointed?"

"I honestly thought you meant something sexy. But yeah, I'd love to get out of the house."

His upper lip curled a little. "Damn it, now I want to do sexy things."

She giggled. "Later?"

"One hundred percent yes."

They left the house, and she climbed onto his back. He carried her down, helping her off and onto the floor. She loved the way he could swing her across the steel branches. It almost felt like they were flying.

They walked hand-in-hand to the marketplace. There wasn't anyone there, and although it was between meals, she was used to seeing people milling around–either the bears working in the kitchen, Anke and Zeger in the little store, or Adriana and Celeste in the nail salon.

Granted, the store run by the wolf couple had been closed for remodeling for the last month, but she'd still seen them around.

"Why's it so deserted?" she asked.

"Because," Neo said.

He walked up to the store and stopped in front of the tarps that had been hung up to keep the dust out of the cafeteria. She watched him curiously as he gripped the edge of tarp and then met her gaze. She was about to ask him what he was doing when he jerked the tarp down, and the clips that held it up went flying. He moved across the storefront, pulling the tarp as he went, revealing the remodeled store.

Then she gasped.

A sign above an arched doorway read, "Dani's Cosmetics."

Neo finished pulling the tarp away, then reached inside the doorway and turned on the light.

The overhead lights illuminated a store between Anke and Zeger's place and the nail salon, with doorways on each side that led to the other stores. Neo held out his hand and she put hers in it, still too surprised to speak. She followed him inside the small store, with shelf-lined walls, and two makeup stations with padded stools and lighted mirrors.

"So," Neo said as he led her to one of the makeup stations and pushed gently on her shoulder so she'd sit. "I know how much you love doing makeup, and since you've been with me, you've done a few makeovers, but it's not the same as coming to a place every day."

She stared at him, unable to articulate how sweet she thought his gesture was. She was so overwhelmed she was tongue-tied.

He frowned. "Sweetheart? You can change anything you want. I just went off photos from the cosmetics store where you worked, but you can make it your own. I... shit. You don't like it?"

Startled, she realized he was mistaking her silence for unhappiness. Launching herself from the stool, she hugged him fiercely, happy tears spilling down her cheeks. "It's amazing! I love it so much!" She kissed his neck and then his cheek before finding his lips and pressing hers against them.

He pulled from the kiss, one arm banded around her waist and holding her close. He brushed the tears from her cheeks. "You do? Really? You were so quiet."

"Sorry, I've just never had anyone build me a store before."

He grinned. "I want you to be happy."

"I am. I mean, I was happy before, but this is over the top."

He slowly relaxed his hold, and she turned to look around

the little shop. She couldn't believe she had her own store now, with displays to set up and shelves to organize. And makeovers!

"I hope you don't mind the secret I had to keep. I wanted it to be a surprise."

"I promise there isn't a soul on this planet more surprised than me right now."

She walked around the store and stopped at the makeup stations, flipping on the lighted mirrors. Peering at her reflection, she brushed under her eyes with her fingertips and sniffled with a smile.

"I can't believe you did this for me," she said as she straightened.

"You quit the cosmetics store for me, Dani. Even though you weren't saying it in so many words, I know you were feeling like you didn't have a purpose. You kept finding projects in the house, but that's not what you really wanted to do. I'd be an idiot not to see how much you wanted to get back to doing makeup."

She walked to him and hugged him with a broad smile. "You're the best thing that's ever happened to me, Neo. I love you from the bottom of my heart."

"I love you, too, sweetheart. You're my whole world." He reached to a top shelf and handed her a spiral-bound note-book with a red ribbon on it. She pulled the ribbon and smiled at the gold embossed letters on the caramel-colored leather that read, "Appointments."

"I think you thought of everything," she said.

"I tried, believe me." He chuckled and kissed her. "The only thing I didn't do was order your supplies. Anke and Zeger can help you with that, or I can take you shopping so you can stock the shelves."

She let out a deep sigh as she looked around the room,

stopping her gaze on her sexy soulmate. "Just when I think I can't be any happier, you outdo yourself. I can't believe you did this for me. I'm overwhelmed and excited."

"I'm glad."

She rose onto her toes and kissed him. "Did I say thanks?"

"You did."

"And I told you I love you?"

"You did that, too."

She rolled her eyes in thought. "Did I tell you I want to go home so we can rock each other's worlds?"

His gorilla hooted softly. Neo swung her up into his arms and strode toward the doorway, stopping only long enough to turn off the lights. "You didn't, but I'm so fucking glad you did."

Khyle sat in the makeup chair, peering at himself in the lighted mirror.

"What do you think?" Dani asked as she placed the last bottle of coconut face cleanser on a shelf.

"It's awesome, D."

"I can tell you're enamored with the mirrors," she said with a chuckle. Breaking down the box, she folded it flat and dropped it to the floor with the others.

"Well, I like what I see," he said. "Can't help that I'm hot."

"Ew."

Khyle laughed. "So when's your first client?"

Dani blew out a breath. "No one's signed up yet."

"It's only been a couple days since you opened, though. They'll come." He nodded sagely, all confidence and bravado. Exactly what she always thought of her brother. He'd left the herd to save it. The herd was now Crew, Ford, Avi, and

Grey–who'd moved into the farm and were still working for Dexter and the construction company.

While Khyle still worked at the apartment complex, which was scheduled to be finished soon, he'd moved into the park and lived underground with the gorillas. Because of Dani, Atticus felt it was best for Khyle to be with them instead of with another shifter group. He'd moved into a spare bedroom in August's house, and the two seemed to be becoming fast friends.

She smiled at her brother. "I'm glad you're here."

"Me, too. I mean I hate what happened to the herd, but I'm glad the guys are still around. It would suck if they'd had to relocate."

She hummed. "Dad would've missed them. And me, too. They're family."

"They're happy."

"Have they decided who's going to be alpha?"

He raised his brows. "Yes and no."

"What do you mean?"

"They all want to be alpha, so they decided to let fate decide."

"Fate? Like a coin toss or rock-paper-scissors?"

He snorted so loudly he coughed. "No, D. They've decided that whoever finds his soulmate first becomes alpha. They'll move through the ranks in the same way–the next guy will be the second-in-command and so on. Not that it really matters, there are only four of them, and they'll most likely make major decisions by voting."

"You miss being in the herd?"

"Yeah. But I feel good about being here. Even if I do have to hang out with that damn moose."

Tank–the resident moose, whose nickname was short for "Cantankerous"–was exactly as his name described him. All grumpy, all the time. Because Khyle was a horse shifter, he didn't really fit in with the other shifters, so he spent time during the VIP tours with the normal animals–giraffe, rhinos, antelope, and Tank in a huge paddock.

"I kinda feel like I was meant to be here, you know?" Khyle said.

"I totally do."

"Oh, sorry!" A feminine voice said. "I didn't know you had company."

Dani looked at the door where a pretty blonde stood. "It's not company, just my brother."

"Rude," Khyle said.

Dani gave him a swat on his shoulder as she walked past him to shake the woman's hand. "Hi, I'm Dani. Can I help you?"

"My name is Sarah. I was invited to go out dancing with some of the pack, and I thought that maybe you might have time to do my eyes? I can't ever get the eyeliner to look decent."

"Oh, I'd love to!" Dani said. She tried to tamp down her enthusiasm, but she couldn't stop the big grin from spreading across her face.

"Really? That's awesome, thank you."

"Come on in and have a seat," Dani said.

"That's my cue," Khyle said.

"You don't have to leave on my account," Sarah said.

"It's nothing against you, I can just smell that the barbecue ribs some of the bears were working on are finally done in the kitchen, and I was told there would be a slab with my name on it."

"Thanks for stopping by," Dani said.

"Sure thing, D. See ya."

He exited the shop, and Dani turned to Sarah. "Just your eyes?"

"Do you have time to do my whole face?"

"Absolutely. When are you leaving?"

"An hour."

"Is this what you're wearing?"

Sarah looked down at the simple cotton shirt she'd paired with jeans. "It's not okay?"

Dani gave her a long look and said, "There's a perfect top in the shop next door. Come on."

Anke and Zeger had closed for the night, but Dani had their permission to go into the shop anytime. She took Sarah back to the clothing and found the top she'd considered getting for herself. It was a cute white sweater with slits down the sleeves from shoulder to wrist that were loosely tied closed with ribbon. Sarah took off her shirt and put on the sweater. They walked back into the makeup shop, and Dani stood next to her while she looked at herself in the lighted mirror.

"It's really pretty," Sarah said. She tugged self-consciously on the hem of the top that showed a bit of her belly.

"You've got a great figure," Dani said. "Guys love curves."

"None I know," she said, rolling her eyes.

"Your soulmate will, though."

Sarah went quiet, and Dani busied herself with first cleaning her face, then applying moisturizer and primer, before matching her skin tone for a light layer of foundation.

"Hey, damn," Sarah said as Dani applied a silky-feeling translucent powder to her skin.

"Damn good or damn bad?" Dani asked.

"Good, really good. I don't think my skin's ever looked so nice."

"Aw, I'm glad." She picked up a shadow palette and said, "Do you want something soft and feminine or more like a smokey eye?"

"Dramatic. I think?"

Dani smiled. "You've got beautiful eyes; you can definitely have a smokey eye and look dramatic."

"Then go to it, girl."

Dani got to work, listening as Sarah talked about being a wolf shifter and one of only two unmated females in the pack. "Why are there so few females?"

"I don't know," she said. "My dad said that predator shifters have more male children than females, but he never said why he thought that."

"Must make it tough to date."

"Shifters don't date. Well, not really," Sarah said. "I mean, if I wanted to have a baby and I didn't want to wait for my soulmate, I might ask Joss to set up a meeting with an eligible male from another pack who was interested in having a child but not becoming mated."

Dani frowned. "People do that?"

"Shifters do. If they want to have kids but don't want to mate with anyone but their soulmate. I could also decide I wanted to just mate with someone and start a family, but we still wouldn't date. Not like humans do. Our families would meet, and we'd spend time together, fuck around and see if we're compatible."

"It sounds kind of sad. No offense." Dani put down the eyeliner and picked up the false lashes.

"I'm not offended. Some people don't like to wait for fate. Especially shifters who don't believe in soulmates. I happen to believe that my soulmate is out there somewhere, I just haven't met him yet."

"Maybe tonight."

Sarah snorted. "I highly doubt that, but there's nothing wrong with a little bit of hope, I guess."

Dani finished applying the lashes, then swiped highlighter and blush on her skin, adding a pale lip gloss as a final touch.

Dani swiveled the stool around so Sarah could see her reflection.

Her eyes went wide. "Holy shit!" She leaned forward and stared at herself.

"Holy shit good? I hope."

"Definitely. I don't think I've ever looked this good! You're a miracle worker."

Sarah turned and hugged Dani.

"Aw," Dani said with a chuckle. "I'm glad you like my work."

"Like it? I freaking love it. I'm going to tell everyone to come see you. Thank you so much!"

"You're welcome. I'm so glad you stopped by."

"Me, too. Hey, can I get some of that facial cleanser that smells like coconuts? I love it."

Dani pulled a bottle off the shelf and handed it to her after she scanned it into the tablet to keep track of stock. "Here you go. It's my favorite."

"Thanks again," Sarah said.

"Good luck tonight," Dani said.

Sarah waved and left, leaving Dani alone in the shop. She smiled to herself as she cleaned up, thinking how happy it made her to make people happy.

"Hey sweetheart," Neo said from the doorway. "You ready to close for the night?"

"You bet," she said.

"You look like you were thinking something really good. Maybe about me?" He wiggled his brows suggestively.

She laughed and turned off the mirror. She walked past the counter where she placed the tablet in a drawer and locked it, pocketing the key. As she reached the doorway, she turned off the lights and then kissed her soulmate.

"I'm always thinking sexy things about you. You're irresistible."

"So are you."

She told him about Sarah and how good she felt helping her out.

"I'm glad she stopped by," Neo said.

They linked hands and walked away from the marketplace, heading toward the gorillas' private living area. "Me, too."

She stopped once they were inside the area and the door was shut. He looked down at her, giving her a curious smile. "Everything okay, love?"

She didn't answer right away, but looked around the area at the homes on fake trees made of steel, the dark floor and painted walls that made her feel like they weren't in New Jersey underneath a safari park, but were somewhere wild and free. So much had changed in the last month since she'd met Neo and learned the secret of his people and her own family. But the herd had recovered from the loss of two members, Khyle was fitting in with the shifters, and her parents were getting ready to go on their first vacation in twenty years once the apartment complex was finished.

"I'm so happy." She looked up at him.

"Me, too, sweetheart."

"I mean that from the bottom of my heart. I thought I was happy before, but it's a shadow of what I feel now. You're everything to me. I'm so glad for the events that fell into place to bring us together. I didn't know soulmates were real, but I'm glad you're mine."

He pulled her close, his eyes darkening and his gorilla hooting happily.

"Sweetheart, I'm so glad you're mine, too. The other half of my heart. Sweet, sexy soulmate. Love of my life."

He kissed her, sending her senses reeling, and then he carried her up to their home, where they chased the night from the sky with their love, and fell asleep, sated and happy, in each other's arms.

She couldn't believe that a trip to the safari park had brought her so much happiness. She was thankful for the twist of fate that had brought her and Neo together, and she couldn't wait to see what the future would bring.

AVAILABLE NOW IN THE ASHLAND
PRIDE SERIES
SEDUCING SAMANTHA (BOOK ONE)

www.rebutlerauthor.com

CONTACT THE AUTHOR

Website: http://www.rebutlerauthor.com
Email: rebutlerauthor@gmail.com
Facebook: www.facebook.com/R.E.ButlerAuthorPage

Every Sunset Forever

Every Blissful Moment

Every Heavenly Moment

Every Miraculous Moment

Every Angelic Moment

The Necklace Chronicles

The Tribe's Bride

The Gigolo's Bride

The Tiger's Bride

The Alpha Wolf's Mate

The Jaguar's Bride

The Author's True Mate

Norlanian Brides

Paoli's Bride

Warrick's Bride

Dex's Bride

Norlanian Brides Volume One

Villi's Bride

Dero's Bride

Saber Chronicles

Saber Chronicles Volume One (Books One - Four)

Sable Cove

Must Love Familiars

Tails

Memory

Mercy

Emberly

AnnaRose

Uncontrollable Shift

The Alpha's Christmas Mate

The Dragon's Treasured Mate

The Bear's Reluctant Mate

The Leopard Twins' Christmas Mate

Vampire Beloved

Want

Need

Ache

Were Zoo

Zane

Jupiter

Win

Justus

Devlin

Kelley

Auden

Tayme

Joss

Neo

Wiccan-Were-Bear

A Curve of Claw

A Flash of Fang

A Price for a Princess

A Bond of Brothers

A Bead of Blood

A Twitch of Tail

A Promise on White Wings

A Slash of Savagery

Awaken a Wolf

Daeton's Journey

A Dragon for December

A Muse for Mishka

The Wiccan-Were-Bear Series Volume One

The Wiccan-Were-Bear Series Volume Two

The Wiccan-Were-Bear Series Volume Three

A Wish for Their Woman

Wilde Creek

Volume One (Books 1 and 2)

Volume Two (Books 3 and 4)

Volume Three (Books 5 and 6)

The Hunter's Heart (Book Seven)

The Beta's Heart (Book Eight)

The Wolf's Mate

The Wolf's Mate Book 1: Jason & Cadence

The Wolf's Mate Book 2: Linus & The Angel

The Wolf's Mate Book 3: Callie & The Cats

The Wolf's Mate Book 4: Michael & Shyne

The Wolf's Mate Book 5: Bo & Reika

The Wolf's Mate Book 6: Logan & Jenna

The Wolf's Mate Book 7: Lindy & The Wulfen

~

Available Now in the Ashland Pride Series: Seducing Samantha (Book One)

Elementary school music teacher Samantha Thomas moved to Ashland to start her life over. What she didn't expect was for her ex-husband to follow her to Ashland to take over the vacant principal job at her school. After some clever plotting by one of her students, she meets the gorgeous Grant Fallon and accepts a date with him. On the way home, her car gets stuck and she finds herself face to face with another gorgeous man asking her for a date – Grant's brother, Aaron. How will Sam decide between Grant and Aaron, when both men fill her with desire?

Mountain lions Grant and Aaron Fallon grew up believing that love was not meant for their kind. When their pride left their former home in Pennsylvania and settled in Ashland, Indiana, they were suddenly able to live their lives however they wanted, without the threat of the female lions holding them back. When they realize that they both want Samantha, they decide to follow their instincts and share her. Can two brothers share a mate? Will Samantha want to be shared?

This book contains m/f/m interaction between two mountain lion males who won't let anyone harm their mate and a woman with a heavy heart. Expect plenty of hot sex, a little danger, handcuffs, shifting, and liberal use of the word 'mine'.

Printed in Great Britain
by Amazon

62246026R00088